A

Crossworder's

Gift

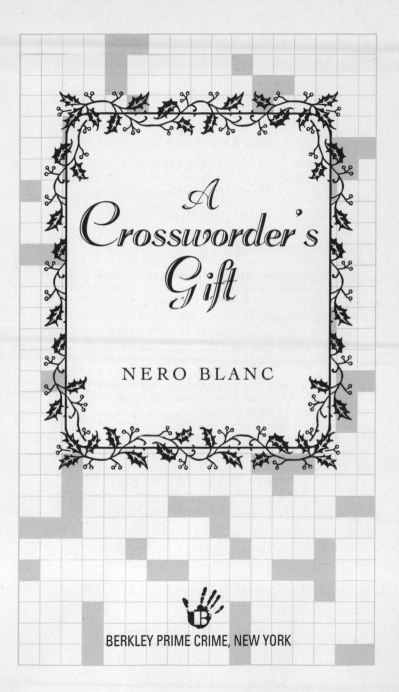

A Crossworder's Gift

NERO BLANC

BERKLEY PRIME CRIME, NEW YORK

A Berkley Prime Crime Book
Published by The Berkley Publishing Group
A division of Penguin Group (USA) Inc.
375 Hudson Street
New York, New York 10014

PRINTING HISTORY
Berkley Prime Crime hardcover edition / October 2003
Berkley Prime Crime trade paperback edition / October 2004

The Library of Congress has already catalogued the Berkley Prime Crime
hardcover edition under LCCN: 2003057932.

PRINTED IN THE UNITED STATES OF AMERICA

10   9   8   7   6   5   4   3   2   1

A Letter from Nero Blanc

Dear Reader,

With our second short story collection, we've decided to continue our travels: One tale is set on the sunny side of Saint Lucia in the Caribbean—a far cry from the cold of many folk's winter holiday locales. One will carry you to Montreal during the fabulous—and very icy—Festival of Lights. The title story unfolds in Las Vegas on the week following Thanksgiving. One backdrop is the Grand Canyon during a particularly perilous New Year's Eve; and one returns to our cozy, snowbound haunt of Massachussetts.

We're also supporting a cherished cause this year—literacy—and have auctioned off the chance to name a character in one of our tales in order to support a number of organizations addressing the issue. They are: the Miami Valley Literacy Council, Project READ, Womanline's ABC's for Babies, the Back Pack Project, and the Kettering City Schools Even Start Program. We thank them for their fine work, and we thank Books & Co. in Dayton, Ohio, for asking us to participate.

As always, we love hearing from you, and invite you to send your messages through our website: crosswordmysteries.com, where you'll find information about other Nero Blanc books as well as additional puzzles.

So, curl up with a cup of cocoa, sharpen your pencils, and enjoy your holiday "visits"!

Steve and Cordelia
aka Nero Blanc

The authors dedicate a percentage of their earnings from *A Crossworder's Gift* to The ECS Beacon Center* in Philadelphia, Pennsylvania.

---

*The ECS Beacon Center is a school-based community center providing academic and recreational programs for children, teens, and adults. Episcopal Community Services (ECS) is a not-for-profit social service agency that has been helping people of all faiths for more than 130 years. For information, visit The Beacon Center at www.bestbeacon.org or ECS at www.ecs1870.org.

ANNABELLA Graham couldn't decide who "Jolly Roger Conner" most resembled: Ernest Hemingway, Walt Whitman, Karl Marx—or Santa Claus. Balanced atop his large and leonine head was a red felt Christmas hat with green holly-leaf trim and a white tassel dangling from the peaked tip. This, added to his expansive girth, snow white hair and beard, voluminous red shorts, and a T-shirt reading X-MAS MARKS THE SPOT—PIRATE'S COVE MARINA AND WATERING HOLE—ST. LUCIA, tipped the scales in favor of Santa. However, the man stood behind a long mahogany and bamboo bar polishing a martini glass, which seriously diminished the warm and fuzzy feel normally associated with the jolly old elf.

Seated at the aforementioned bar and beachside eatery, "Belle"—as her friends called her—and her husband, Rosco

3

Polycrates, had just been served two very colorful tropical drinks by the S. Claus/Whitman/Marx/Hemingway-esque owner of the establishment. That fact, combined with the weather, view, and ambience—an eighty-five-degree afternoon gracing the limpid, azure waters of Marigot Bay, and a sound system jingling Christmas carols, steel-band style, rather than the chilly riffs concerning snow and reindeer that always signified Yuletide in Belle and Rosco's native New England—curtailed the candidacies of Whitman and Marx, as well as Santa Claus.

As far as Belle knew, those men had not been given to winter holidays lolling on a palm-tree-dotted sand spit, snorkeling gear close by, rum drinks in hand, and pleasure craft at the ready—which brought her to Papa Hemingway, and the *Key Largo/Old Man and the Sea,* vision that kept dancing, like coconut-covered sugar plums, in her head.

"Yep . . . Ate 'em up, they did!" Conner now insisted in a dramatic and piratey tone that had a fair amount of Ireland in its subtler shadings. "Just like that!" For emphasis, he snapped his chubby fingers, and an Amazon green parrot, waddling around on a driftwood perch beside the bar, added a loud and bossy, "Bottoms up, maties," as if the statement had been cause for a toast. In fact, many of Pirate's Cove's patrons polished off what was left of their "2-4-1 Happy Hour" drinks upon hearing the bird's pronouncement.

It was becoming clear to Belle that Conner was no slouch when it came to a larger-than-life personality, and that he relished having a captive audience—in this case, a couple from Newcastle, Massachusetts, recently arrived and fair game for tall tales or fish tales or yarns of ancient derring-do.

"What do you mean, 'ate them up'?" Belle asked.

"Just what I said, my honey-haired maiden!" Conner's voice boomed; his broad forearm traced an expansive sweep. "Cannibals, they was. Cannibals, for good or ill. Of course, this was nearly four hundred years ago . . . a good hundred years *after* the good Señor Chris Columbus discovered our little island of Saint Lucia." He leaned across the bar, bringing his nose within a foot of Belle's, then lowered his voice into a rumbling drawl. "The British settlers landed in 1605. Sixty-seven of 'em they was, and only nineteen escaped. The Caribs killed the rest of 'em . . . and had 'em for dinner! Yum . . . yum . . . yum!"

"That's horrible."

"Aye, that it is, my little miss. And it gets worse. 'Cause in 1638 another party of English came over from Saint Kitts way . . . Pretty spot this, they says to themselves, pleasing terrain, mountain mists . . . good for growing comestibles: sugar cane, plantains, et cetera, et cetera . . . But they met with the very same fate: people stew! Stick that in your pipe and smoke it, all ye landlubbers."

"Oh, Roger, stop! You'll be scaring these nice people." The woman speaking had just entered from the tile-covered veranda. Dressed island style in flip-flops and a batik sundress, she was carrying a damp towel, and snorkel and fins in one hand; with the other, she pulled off her dark glasses, extended her hand, and smiled. It was a bright and cheerful expression, full of warmth and welcome. "I'm Elaine. This is my husband, Joe."

Joe also smiled in greeting. He was similarly equipped, and had a picnic cooler he'd just carried from the dinghy tied to the end of the pier. "That's our boat out there—" He pointed farther into the harbor to a white-hulled sailboat newly moored there. "We've been snorkeling in Anse Cochon—"

"Joe and Elaine," interjected Roger with another theatrical and all-inclusive gesture. "They spend so much time in Saint Lucia, they've become honorary *Looshans*. Ask anyone hereabouts."

Elaine turned her sunny face toward him. "You shouldn't be frightening folks, Roger, with all these nasty stories—"

"The truth's the truth," he retorted in a sulky if not altogether abashed tone. "And what about the three Spanish galleons sunk where yon beach now stands?"

"Rumor, Roger. Only rumor."

"Or the German U-boat that crept into the inner harbor? Or the pirates that patrolled these waters?"

Elaine shook her head. "I'll accept the U-boat and the tales of piracy, but not the galleons, and some of that other nonsense. None of us do." She glanced at the other regulars, then returned her attention to Belle. "Is this your first visit to the island?"

"Yes, we—"

"Stop!" the barkeep barked as he held his hands high in the air. All neighboring conversation ceased. A number of patrons chuckled; Joe and Elaine shook their heads; clearly, everyone except Rosco and Belle had witnessed this exhibition before.

Conner removed his elf hat and reverently placed it in front of him. "The Great Roger Conner-ronnor-bonnor-ella will now use his mystical psychic powers, and read the fair lady's cocktail napkin. The likes of such clairvoyance you have never before witnessed in all your born days!"

He lifted Belle's drink from the napkin and set it aside while the parrot squawked another insistent: "Bottoms up, maties!"

Conner studied the napkin and lowered his voice, giving it an otherworldly lilt as he placed his meaty paw above Belle's head. "With your permission, I will commence with age and weight . . . The fair damsel here is a little upward of thirty years old and weighs one hundred and twelve pounds—"

"The age isn't overly specific," Rosco interjected with a chuckle.

"Damsels require a certain *flexibility,*" Conner countered as he moved his hand toward Rosco. "And her first mate would be thirty-eight, methinks . . . and weighing in at . . ." Conner paused for dramatic effect. ". . . one hundred and seventy-three pounds."

"Seventy-*three?*" Rosco groused. "I was one hundred seventy-*one* last time I checked."

"Silence, please, the Great Roger Conner-ronnor-bonnor-ella is only getting warmed up. I see it all clearly now; you were married last week and sailed into Marigot Bay with the high tide at high noon."

"Not quite," Rosco answered. Conner raised a skeptical eyebrow.

Belle grinned. "We were married last year, and flew in on a 737 from Massachusetts two hours ago."

"No interruptions," Conner objected. "That was to be the Amazing Roger's next deduction."

This brought hearty laughter from the regulars. Conner turned to them:

"So, ladies and gents gathered on this convivial December afternoon, we have some landlubbers amongst us . . . renters of one of the pleasant cottages perched upon yon hillside, perchance . . . Perchance nigh to the fair Elaine's and the lordly Señor Joe's?" He turned back to Rosco. "Stop, don't answer the question! I see it all plainly on the face of the napkin."

Rosco had nodded, but Conner ignored the reaction as he continued his performance, regarding the cocktail napkin with renewed intensity.

"Hmmm, I note that our male visitor is a member of the illustrious law-enforcement clan . . . in short, a policeman." Before Rosco could protest, Conner switched to Belle's napkin and said, "And you, my dear, despite your angelic appearance, are a mathematician?"

This brought a quick laugh from husband and wife; Elaine and Joe and the rest of the patrons joined in, believing that once again Jolly Roger Conner had missed the mark by a mile.

"Bottoms up, maties!" the parrot screamed, then flapped onto the bar and began striding toward them with a cocky and aggressive swag.

Rosco eyed the determined bird with some apprehension. "He doesn't bite, does he?"

"Who? Jimmy Bungs?" Conner rubbed his beard and considered his answer as the parrot approached. "That's a good question. He *does* have his favorites, and he can be a nasty cuss when he puts his mind to it . . . A *Jimmy Bungs* for ye landsmen and lubbers is slang for a member of the ship's crew, and our Jim can be just as perverse and particular as any sailor worth his salt."

The bird stopped in front of Rosco and ripped the corner from the napkin under his beer. Opting to keep a safe distance, Rosco slid his bar stool back while the parrot went into his now familiar patter: "Bottoms up, maties."

Conner swatted at the parrot with a bar towel and said, "Put a lid on it, Jimmy. We're conducting business here."

"Cheerio, dumbbell," was the bird's swift reply. Then he waddled a little farther down the bar, hopped onto Belle's shoulder, and began to nibble affectionately at her earlobe.

"Ahhh, now you're lookin' like the Pirate Queen of Saint *Loosha*," Conner cackled. "I gather by your reaction to my psychic powers of observation I was in error with my cop and math geek analysis?"

"Believe it or not," Rosco said, "I was once in the police force . . . *Once*. Now I'm a private investigator. Belle, my wife, is the crossword puzzle editor at the *Evening Crier*. It's a newspaper in Massachusetts."

Conner stiffened slightly but, after a second, rejoined with a boisterous: "Well, well, well! I think you'll find there are more than a few crossword fiends, addicts, and inveterate word game veterans gathered around these turquoise depths . . . Yes-in-dee-dee . . ." He looked around the room, pointing as he spoke. "Aussies: Gerda and Mike Menzies off the catamaran *Roo Two;* Brits: Carlotta and Noel; that's their ketch *In Sou Sea Ant* with the black hull; Brian Joseffson—aka 'the Brain'—of the *Leopard Sun* . . . and you've already met Elaine and Joe . . ." Conner turned back to Belle. "In defense of my initial reading of the napkins, you must admit that your vocation deals in numbers and symmetry—i.e., you're a numbers person." Conner smiled broadly, and again raised his voice. "So, the Great Roger Conner-ronnor-bonnor-ella is vindicated! Once again he stupefies the nonbelievers!"

"Cheerio, dumbbell," Jimmy Bungs announced again, then followed it with a series of squawks that duplicated mocking laughter.

Conner frowned. "Creatures like our Mr. Bungs are either drawn to menfolk." He directed the comment to Rosco rather than Belle. "Or they're drawn to womenfolk; but I've never met an Amazon Green who liked 'em both. As you can see, Jimmy is most definitely a ladies man."

"Well, he is kind of cute," Belle said, peering at the bird out of the corner of her eye, then tilting her head playfully, forcing the parrot to chase after her dangling earring with short, gentle pecks from his beak. "And a bit of a flirt."

"He appears to have a limited vocabulary," Rosco added in an unsuccessful attempt to outdo the bird.

Conner laughed. "You're right about that, my friend. For an old-timer, Jimmy hasn't picked up more than those two phrases . . . besides a small selection of *sailors' prayers,* if you know what I mean. He can be downright raunchy when he starts in on his favorite oaths, though he seems to keep that chatter under wraps when in the company of the fairer sex."

"How old is he?" Belle asked as she fed Jimmy the orange slice from her drink.

"No telling, really, but definitely over fifty. I inherited our Mr. Bungs from an erstwhile fishing compatriot. A hunter after sunken treasure who called this harbor his true abode . . ."

It was Carlotta and Noel who continued the story, tag teaming as they supplied the facts. "A tough go, it was, when the old man died . . . Digger Bonnet was his name. Came from Antigua, originally, by way of Martinique, but he was a Marigot fixture long before we first arrived . . . And he gave up the ghost right here where we're sitting . . . Fell face first onto the bar . . ." They looked to Conner, who continued the story:

"And Jimmy there just squawked, gave Digger a nasty look, and strolled to the other end of the bar, where he began eating peanuts out of a dish . . . He's been with me ever since."

"Does that happen often around here?" Rosco asked. "People dropping dead at beachside bars?"

"I've owned the place for over thirty years," Conner said. "And I heard plenty of stories from the previous owners. But in answer: Nope, that's the only time it's happened to me."

"It's an occurrence you wouldn't easily forget."

"Truer words . . ."

"And Bonnet was a real treasure hunter?" Belle asked.

This time it was Gerda who answered. "He certainly talked an impressive game, didn't he, Mike? Absolutely insisted the tale of sunken galleons was true, and that he'd found a cache of Spanish doubloons—"

Roger interrupted. "How else to explain how the man put food on the table? He never worked a day in his life, unless you call scuba diving work." He grinned although Belle could see the jovial expression was forced. Discussing his friend's death was obviously not easy. "You know, you and Digger shared something in common—besides Jimmy's questionable affection . . . Bonnet was a real crossword junkie, he was. A man who liked riddles, *double entendres,* puns, spoonerisms, anagrams . . ."

"That he did," Brian agreed.

"So, Mr. Bonnet died a wealthy man?" Rosco mused after a moment.

"Like they say," Conner said, "ya can't take it with you."

"Was the cause of death natural?" Rosco asked, unable to suppress his inquisitive nature—even on vacation. "Or was someone after the loot?"

"Foul play? Is that what you're inferring?" Conner asked. "Digger was nearly ninety when he passed away. The only foul play is spelled F-O-W-L, and Jimmy has a market on that."

"So, that must make Jimmy the richest personality on Saint Lucia," Belle said.

Conner shook his head. "There wasn't money enough in Digger's pockets to pay for the rum in front of him when he keeled over. And to this day, there hasn't been a trace of anything else of value. Not a savings account. Not a bank box. Nothing."

Gerda and Mike Menzies joined in. "Some of us think old Bonnet grew odd toward the end and scuttled his purported bounty by dumping it outside the bay . . . Others are convinced he buried it on the island somewhere—"

"And then there's the third camp," added Elaine with a laugh, "who don't believe there was as much as one red cent to begin with."

"And which camp are you in, Roger?" Rosco asked.

Conner shrugged. "I have to admit, old Digger talked a good game. Once in a blue moon, he'd turn up when I was locking up the doors here, and give me a quick glimpse of something he'd insist was a piece of eight—Spanish gold—or a stone he'd swear up and down was an uncut emerald taken from the mines of Brazil . . . But he'd make me promise to keep my mouth shut for fear the government would be askin' for too big of a slice of his briny pie . . . I'd say Digger must have had a nest egg somewhere. But then again . . ." Conner shrugged. "I'll tell you this, if there is such a thing as hidden treasure, there's only one person who knows where it might be, and he's not talkin' to nobody."

"Who's that?"

"He's sitting right there on your sweetie's shoulder."

"The bird?" Rosco said incredulously.

Jimmy Bungs flapped irate wings, stretched his neck, and snapped at Rosco, who jumped back just before the powerful beak came in contact with his ear.

Conner laughed. "Oh, and another thing, he doesn't like to be called 'the bird.' "

"So I gathered."

BY the time the sun had begun to set, Belle and Rosco had returned to their rented bungalow, situated halfway up the verdant hillside, overlooking the sailboats and pleasure yachts that dotted Marigot Bay. The trade winds had cooled the evening to a comfortable seventy-five degrees, and lights were twinkling on in the houses and cottages on the opposite slope. The couple stood arm in arm on the veranda beholding the tranquil scene.

"I wish we had sailed into this harbor, as Roger had imagined," Belle murmured, "rather then arriving by plane."

"That's a long trip from Massachusetts. I'd be greener than Jimmy Bungs right now."

"You know what I mean, Rosco. Wouldn't it be romantic to drift in by sea—under canvas at sunset. Watching the famous 'green flash' in all its glory."

Rosco gave her a light kiss, then put on a Jolly Roger Conner accent. "Aye, my little wench, you mean like the wooden-legged pirates of old sailing under the skull and crossbones, cutlasses clenched between our teeth and a bottle of rum to ward off the night chill."

"It's amazing to think that we left all that ice and snow in Newcastle this morning; and a few hours later were ensconced in an island bungalow: coconut palms, banana trees, the Caribbean spreading all around . . . I guess there's something to be said for the efficiency of modern transportation—"

"As long as your idea of transportation comes with jet propulsion and wings and *not* a mainsail . . . Because, the only *cruising* I want is the kind where there's a steward in a starched white uniform with white gloves and a silver tray; serving me hors d'oeuvres on the fantail . . . None of this trimming the yardarms for me. I'll leave that to salty buccaneers like Jolly Roger."

"Do you think that was true? All his talk about cannibals, and a pirate being the first European to settle on the island?"

"You mean old leg-of-wood *Jambe de Bois,* François Le Clerc? I'm sure it's true. You could see Pigeon Island, where

Roger said Le Clerc set himself up, when we flew in. Seemed a logical spot for a buccaneer: easy to defend, with a nice high vantage point . . . What I found fishy, though, was the Digger Bonnet tale. If Roger truly believed his onetime buddy had buried treasure nearby, why would he spend his time mixing drinks? Why isn't he out looking for it?"

Belle thought. "Maybe he *has* found it, and isn't telling anyone."

"I don't know, Belle . . . Given Conner's fondness for the dramatic, I'd say the entire fable is merely fodder for tourists."

"The others seemed to believe it."

"Gerda, Carlotta, and all?"

"Hmmm-hmmm . . ."

"I'm not so sure. I think the Pirate's Cove regulars like humoring Conner, like egging him on. Besides, remember what Elaine said? That some folks doubt the man had one red cent when he died?" Rosco stepped back from the railing, sat on a rattan love seat, and placed his feet on the matching ottoman. The first star was just beginning to show itself. Belle snuggled up next to him.

"Still . . ." she said, "I find the notion of treasure fascinating. Think of all that's been lost in the sea over the centuries . . . Spanish doubloons, emeralds from South America—"

"Exactly! That's exactly my point. All that's been lost— including many, many people. Another good reason why you'd never catch me out there on the briny, sailing around on some yawl or ketch or something. A hurricane comes along, next thing you know, you're fish food."

"There are no hurricanes in December."

A small black bird with a ruby-colored throat soared down out of the sky and landed on the veranda railing in front of them. He then marched back and forth on the painted wood, and chirped insistently at Belle and Rosco.

"I think he's trying to tell us something, Rosco."

He laughed. " *'Feed me,'* would be my guess."

"You're right." Belle stood and walked into the cottage. "There are some bananas in the fruit basket," she called. "I'll bet he'd like that." She returned with a half-peeled banana and placed it on the railing. None of her movements seemed to frighten the bird in the slightest; instead, he hopped onto the banana and began pecking away. Within a matter of seconds, he was joined by four other red-throated black birds.

"He must have been the advance scout," Rosco observed. "Probably recognized us as easy marks when we deplaned, and has been following us all afternoon; just waiting to make his move."

"So," Belle said as she leaned against the railing only a foot from the feeding birds, "back to hidden treasure."

"Hmmm, why doesn't it surprise me that you're so intrigued by all this malarkey?" he said. He knew full well that his wife couldn't resist the lure of solving a mystery. *Curiosity* might as well have been her middle name.

"Well, of course I'm intrigued," she said. "I used to love to paw through the boxes stored in my grandmother's attic. There was always a chance of finding an old Indian head penny, or buffalo nickel tucked away in some ancient sewing kit. So how could I *not* be fascinated by Bonnet's treasure—"

"Purported treasure." He stood and placed his arms around her. "This is vacation, remember? No sleuthing? Besides, it's kind of nice to be in a place where *finally* people haven't heard about the crimes you've solved, 'Ms. Annabella Graham, Cryptic Queen and Criminologist' . . . I'm looking forward to reading a few books on the beach and forgetting ice, snow, slush, sleet, and W-O-R-K for the entire W-E-E-K."

The birds decided they'd had enough banana, and flew off toward the harbor. Within a few minutes a small gray and brown lizard poked his head around the railing post and checked to see if the coast was clear. Like the birds, he saw no immediate danger in the large humans, and after a moment he crossed the railing to what was left of the fruit and started in on his dinner.

"I guess they would have all starved to death if we hadn't arrived," Rosco said.

"Something tells me that the owners of this place leave food for the wildlife rather than the guests. I'll bet the people who rented this cottage last week never got near the bananas . . . Look." Belle pointed. "Here comes another lizard. This should be good."

"You're expecting a jousting match? Pistols at twenty paces? Épées, maybe?"

"Shhh. I just want to see what they do. I have the feeling this guy isn't in any mood to share."

"That's a lot of snacks for one little guy . . . Let me know when the action starts. I'll work out our itinerary for tomorrow . . ." Rosco began flipping through the Saint Lucia tourist information. "According to this, all that pirate *Jambe de Bois* stuff that Roger fed us was on the mark . . . Hmmm, it says here that Pigeon Island wasn't connected to the mainland back then. That didn't occur until 1971 . . . Anyway, we can hike out there if we want to . . . See where the buccaneers did their conniving . . ."

"These lizards aren't doing anything but staring at each other . . ."

"And the cannibal stories are genuine as well. It seems the French and English swapped ownership of Saint Lucia on a regular basis. I'd gather this necessitated the exchange of a fair amount of buckshot as well—given how fond the French are of the English, and vice versa. Eventually the cannibals were . . . shall we say, eliminated. Or perhaps they just had their fill of white men shooting at each other and decided to hit the road . . . Or in this case, sail off into the sunset."

"Maybe if I pushed this one toward the banana a little?"

"The island changed hands a total of fourteen times in a hundred and fifty years. Can you believe that?"

"This is a real Mexican standoff . . ."

"Statio haud malefidia carinis!"

Belle turned away from the lizards and faced Rosco. "What did you say?"

"I thought that might get your attention. *A safe haven for ships;* it's Saint Lucia's motto. I'll bet it came in handy for the corsair types. You know, throw around a little Latin? Impress the ladies? Make folks think you've got an education? Then go and plunder their vessels?"

Rosco turned to the last page of the tourist publication. His eyes widened slightly, and his brow pinched. Then he closed the newspaper, and slid it to the bottom of a stack of magazines sitting under the side table. The maneuver was more obvious than he'd intended, and Belle immediately recognized its deviousness.

"How about some dinner?" he said in an attempt to cover his activity.

"Rosco?" Belle looked at her watch. "It's not even six-thirty."

"Right."

"What's going on? What's in the newspaper?"

"Oh . . . nothing really . . . skimpy swimsuit ad. Far too revealing, if you ask me. Nothing that would interest you."

She laughed. "I don't believe you for a second." Belle walked over to the stack of magazines, but he stopped her.

"It's only that we're on vacation . . . and . . . well, there's a crossword in the paper, and I thought you'd like to stay away from that while we're away. No W-O-R-K for the W-E-E-K."

"Just because I see a puzzle doesn't mean I have to drop everything I'm doing just to fill it in. I'm not that much of a fanatic."

He glanced down at the stack of newsprint. "You haven't seen this puzzle."

She bent down and retrieved the paper. Realizing it was hopeless, Rosco made no attempt to stop her. On the back page, Belle found the crossword. She opened her eyes wide. "*Digger's Challenge* . . . Let me get my pen."

"I wouldn't want you to 'drop *everything* you're doing just to . . .' Hey! It looks like these lizards are just about ready to go at it, big time."

ACROSS

1. Spark
4. A developing area?
8. Perrault villain
10. Flat fish
11. Tony winner, Arthur
12. Nuclear watchdog; abbr.
14. Baum's land
15. Hosp. rooms
16. LTD & Inc. relative
17. Cab in Cremona
20. "The Hurricane" star
23. Skipper of the Adventure Galley
25. Hire again
26. Mr. Mineo
27. Old salt
28. Right-rain link
30. "Treasure Island" author's monogram
32. Buccaneer's crew, usually
33. "Murder____Death"
35. Latin thing?
37. Pipes down?
39. "____No Evil"
40. Charts
42. Part of AT&T
43. Oafs
44. W. C. Fields', "____a Gift"
46. John Q. to John
47. Barrie villain
48. "The Beggar's____"
50. McQueen or Reeves
53. Snake sound
54. SNAFU
55. "Tell____a Riddle"
56. Bond doctor

DOWN

1. Commonplace
2. Hot coal
3. Enjoyable
4. Price-y insect?
5. Kokomo campus; abbr.
6. Penlight battery
7. Half a suit?
8. Island market places
9. Unscrambler
10. Officer's course; abbr.
13. Line
18. Asparagus unit
19. Moonshine makers
21. Harding or Hamilton
22. Two-stage rocket
24. "This____Your Life"
28. Distribute cutlasses
29. "The____Hawk"; Flynn role
31. Ready-go link
32. Mr. Brooks
33. Plead
34. "Sure!"
36. Caribbean specialty
38. You & me
39. Treasure, often
41. Navigational aids
43. Pirates
45. Retreat
46. "Mayday!"
48. Resistance unit
49. "Easy as____"
51. Panel truck
52. Self

🌴 Digger's Challenge 🌴

T took Belle a little over ten minutes to complete the crossword, which she then handed to Rosco. "What do you think?"

He shrugged. "Nicely done. No errors." He checked his watch. "Ten minutes and eighteen seconds; not a record, but . . . I'm happy to see that you brought your red pen with you—one never knows when an emergency like this might pop up."

Belle grabbed the paper from him. "That's not what I'm talking about, and you know it! I'm talking about the design, and the *title, Digger's Challenge.* What do you think *that* refers to? Definitely, not a clam digger, which means—" Her words were flying out of her mouth so fast she didn't have time to finish one thought before embarking on another. "Because given the skull and crossbones pattern . . . and the clear references to pirates . . . Well, it's obvious there's a secret 'challenge' the solvers are supposed to take."

Rosco retrieved the newspaper. "Do you think you might be reading more into this than there is?" he asked. "Nowhere does the crossword suggest a contest of some sort. Besides, Digger Bonnet is long dead. He couldn't have constructed—"

"Then who did create it?" she demanded. Belle could be stubborn; this was one of those times. She squared her shoulders; her jaw was set. "Okay, if not Bonnet, then—"

"Belle, this is just a little island entertainment in a local handout."

She sighed. "You're right, I guess . . ." Her shoulders hunched in thought. "A little island entertainment, because Roger said Saint Lucia has plenty of crossworders . . ."

"You can find out Monday. The newspaper's office will be closed by now, and tomorrow's Sunday . . ."

Belle squinted her gray eyes and furrowed her brow. It was an expression Rosco had seen many, many times before. He laughed. "I guess the mystery of the constructor *won't* keep until Monday—"

"We can call Roger Conner. He may have some 'insight' on the situation—and even if he doesn't . . ."

Rosco chuckled and walked into the bungalow. Belle followed, and watched her husband chat on the phone for all of thirty seconds.

"Well?" she asked the moment he hung up.

"He was on his way out the door—heading home after 'Happy Hour' and letting the late shift take over. Apparently, Jimmy Bungs gets cranky if he stays at the bar past seven."

"Not a night owl, huh?"

Rosco raised an eyebrow. "I guess not. Roger suggested we stop by his house, since we're in the market for chat and not rum. We take the ferry across the bay, and walk up the hill. His place is on the first dirt road to the right."

They strolled out of their bungalow and headed down the walkway hand in hand. A series of lights bordered the path on either side and shone upon groupings of bird of paradise, hibiscus, and bougainvillea while the stars and a three-quarter moon cast silvery blue shadows among the nodding palm fronds and giant ferns. The tree frogs were beginning their evening ritual; their flutey chirps and whistles floated effortlessly into the night air.

Before leaving the trail, Belle and Rosco stopped, faced each other, and exchanged a long kiss. "This is an awfully romantic spot," she said as they pulled apart.

"Does this mean you want to put this puzzle thing on the back burner?" Rosco asked hopefully. She didn't answer, so he added, "I didn't think so."

The couple retraced their steps to the Pirate's Cove Bar then crossed the beach to the ferry—a minibarge that traversed Marigot Bay at all hours of the day and night. The trip to the far shore took a brief minute of putt-putting among fishing skiffs now deserted until morning.

Once again on shore, they passed the marina's general store and the sleepy police station, and began climbing the hill, turning at the crossroads as per Roger's instructions. After a few hundred yards, Rosco stopped. "This should be his place."

The house didn't appear much larger than the bungalow

Belle and Rosco had rented. It had the same style of windows—*sans* glass panes—a tin roof, and a wraparound veranda, and was surrounded by dense vegetation. However, it was considerably older than their cottage, and time and innumerable tropical storms had left a mark, making the structure look like a fisherman's shack rather than a residence. The door had been left open, but Rosco knocked twice before they stepped inside.

The interior had been decorated à la *Thirties Caribbean Nautical.* Torn fishnets had been slung from the rafters, each adorned with glass and cork floaters, and an assortment of seashells, starfish, and coral fans. The furniture was rattan, and once had been brushed with bright tropical colors, but the paint was now faded to pastel shades, as were the thin and lumpy cushions on the couch and armchairs. Conner was sitting on the couch reading a battered paperback. He didn't appear to have heard their knock, but Jimmy Bungs squawked his habitual "Bottoms up, maties" as the couple passed through the entryway.

Conner glanced up from his book. "Ahhh, there they are! Good old Jimmy; better than a watch dog, he is." He stood and crossed to his guests, extending his hand to Rosco. "Welcome to my humble abode . . . So, you've found the puzzle from the summer issue?"

Belle glanced at the newspaper in her hand. "Gosh! I didn't even notice it was from July . . . I guess the situation wasn't as pressing as I thought."

"And you call yourself a sleuth? Although it doesn't surprise me that you managed to sniff out a five-month-old crossword. Where in the name of Beelzebub did you find it?" Conner took the paper from her and smiled. "And completed without a single error, and with the infamous Belle Graham red pen . . . May I keep this as a souvenir?"

"So, you've heard of my wife?" Rosco asked.

"Oh, indeed." Conner motioned toward a table and chairs by the window. "Please sit . . . Our island may be far away from New England, but we *puzzle people* are well aware of your reputation . . . And the numerous mysterious outrages you've managed to solve, or shall we say resolve?"

Rosco found Jolly Roger's semiserious tone curious. It made him suspect that there was a good deal more to Roger Conner than he'd first surmised. "What surprises me," he said, "is not so much that you're aware of my wife's 'reputation,' as you put it, but the fact that you mentioned none of this earlier. It makes me wonder if—"

Conner held up his large hand. "I can explain this very simply."

Rosco gave him a slight shrug that said, *I'm all ears,* and Conner handed the puzzle back to Belle.

"I guess I'll start at the beginning. It was Digger Bonnet's idea, really. It's just that the poor old guy kicked the bucket before we could get the game off the ground."

"Cheerio, dumbbell," Jimmy Bungs squawked from the far corner of the room. He then flew over to the table and landed on Belle's shoulder.

"Huh," Conner exclaimed, "I haven't seen him fly in years. Not since Digger owned this house. I think Mr. Jimmy Bungs must be in love. He's certainly very fond of you—"

"Digger Bonnet?" Rosco prompted.

"Right. It was Digger's idea to have a contest. Everyone puts ten bucks into a hat. I'm talking U.S., not Eastern Caribbean Dollars . . . And fifteen years ago ten bucks really meant something—meaning the pot was well worth competing for."

Belle and Rosco merely nodded.

"Okay, for their ten bucks they get a sheet of quarter-inch graph paper. We planned to hold the contest at the Pirate's Cove Bar."

Belle was ahead of him. "So, it was intended as a diagramless puzzle?"

"Exactly! That way the contest would last longer. It would've taken some folks all afternoon to figure it out. The bar would have made a killing on drinks, conch fritters, etc. We were going to place the clues on a huge board and flip it over. This way everyone would have been guaranteed to start at the same time . . . First one finished wins the pot. And we planned to do second and third prizes of dinners and beers."

"So what happened?" Rosco asked, not convinced he was hearing the entire truth.

"Like I said, Digger died."

"Bottoms up, maties," Jimmy Bungs added.

Roger Conner ignored him. "The only thing Digger had done was create the dang puzzle grid. I had to invent the clues and solutions later . . . But because the two sections aren't connected"—he pointed at the puzzle in the newspaper—"see, the skull and crossbones have no connecting words—meaning it's virtually impossible for anyone to

solve the crossword as a diagramless . . . I ended up cancel-
ing the entire event."

"Back up a second," Rosco said. "You mean this is the
same grid Digger Bonnet created?"

"Yep."

"How did it get into a newspaper fifteen years later?"

"It's a contest."

"But you said the contest was canceled?" Rosco's forehead
creased in confusion.

Belle also frowned in perplexity. "Roger, I don't think
either one of us is following your explanation—"

"Can I get you a beverage?" Conner asked suddenly. "I've
got Piton, the local beer. Or Ting, which is a carbonated
grapefruit drink."

Belle asked for Ting; Rosco was given a Piton. As soon
as Roger had reseated himself, and appropriate words of
thanks had been expressed, Belle repeated her question.

"Okay . . . Here's what happened: We advertised the contest. Digger created the grid but not the clues or solutions—
then proceeded to die a few days later. End of story: I canceled the proposed competition."

Belle and Rosco waited for Conner to continue. When
he didn't, Rosco's frustration got the better of him. "We
know that. It was fifteen years ago. What we want to know
is: How did the same grid get into this newspaper last July?"

"Right. Well, the next year, the year *after* Digger's death,
I made up words that fit his grid, then put the puzzle in
the newspaper, and mentioned that anyone who solved it
correctly could bring the opus to Pirate's Cove and get a
free sun downer' or whatever beverage suited their fancy.

People came from all over. I told them that Digger had created the crossword—which was partially true; and you all know Digger's remarkable story. I guess folks thought they might get a clue—as it were—to where the loot was sequestered . . . Anyway, I've been rerunning the crossword every summer with new solutions and clues, and the same reward of a free drink for coming up with the correct solution . . ."

Belle let out a small laugh that contained a certain degree of disappointment. "Darn. I felt certain the puzzle was going to lead us to the hidden treasure. It really had me going."

As if in reply, Jimmy Bungs squawked in her ear, and the sound seemed to return Jolly Roger Conner to his previous incarnation. "Aye, as I said earlier, me fair-haired damsel, if Digger Bonnet actually had a pile of lucre, only Jimmy'd be the wiser . . ."

"And this was Bonnet's house?" she asked.

"It was. Left it to me in his will . . . along with everything else." Conner waved a hand, indicating the home and its contents. "Not exactly the trappings of a successful old lobscouser. Like Elaine said, there are plenty of regular visitors who think the whole treasure trove tale was a crock." He sighed slightly. "It makes for a lively story, though."

Belle retrieved the puzzle, and studied it as the parrot hopped from her shoulder onto the table and strode toward Rosco, who automatically slid his chair backward. Jimmy Bungs eyed him, turned back to Belle, pulled the paper from her hands, tossed it onto the table, and returned to her shoulder. Once again he began to nuzzle her earlobe.

"I believe our fine-feathered friend doesn't want to share you with anyone—not even a crossword puzzle," Conner cackled. The newspaper had landed upside down in front of her.

Belle didn't answer for a moment. Instead she kept staring at the paper on the floor. "You know, when you look at the puzzle this way . . . upside down . . ." She raised her eyes toward the beamed ceiling, then lowered them to the word game. "These crossed bones take a shape similar to those support timbers up there . . ." She pointed; both men looked up.

"*I* thought the bones looked like a dumbbell," Rosco said. "But I figured I was being overly sensitive—given the bird's comment."

Jimmy shrieked; obviously, the term "the bird" was still on his no-no list. Rosco drew back, and muttered a placating: "Sorry, Jimbo."

"And look . . ." Belle continued. "With the skull's mouth upside down—at the top rather than the bottom, it looks like that small window up at the peak of your roof line."

Rosco glanced over Belle's shoulder at the puzzle. "That's kind of far-fetched . . ."

"No, no," Conner said excitedly, now standing beside Belle and pointing at the crossword. "See, this 'eye,' next to 16-Down here, it looks exactly like Digger's built-in desk—"

"And the square that's the skull's 'nose' is in the exact position of the television set," Belle added.

"That's not a fifteen-year-old TV," Rosco objected, still failing to see the similarity between the puzzle and the interior design of the bungalow. "It couldn't have been there when Digger designed this crossword grid."

"No, it wasn't. I bought that set last year when Digger's ancient TV died on me. But I put the replacement in the same place."

"Okay"—Rosco pointed to the other eye—"but what's this 'eye' represent? The black space below 18 and 19? There's nothing there. Or"—he looked at Conner—"was something in that position at one time?"

He shook his head. "Nope. Never. I haven't moved a single thing since I moved in. Well, I couldn't move anything. All of this furniture was built by Digger. Most of it's nailed in place."

Belle sighed. "It's just . . . Well, it's amazing how much this upside-down puzzle resembles this space. I felt from the first, it contained some secret . . ."

"Bottoms up, maties," Jimmy Bungs tossed in.

"See, even cute little Jimmy was telling us to reverse the puzzle . . ."

Rosco opted not to comment on Belle's assessment of "cute." Instead he asked Conner, "Do you have a ruler or tape measure?"

"Sure." Conner disappeared into the kitchen, and returned with a yardstick.

Rosco walked over to the far wall and measured the distance between the built-in desk and the television. Conner and Belle followed, and Jimmy flew back to Belle's shoulder. "Four feet, six inches," Rosco said. He moved to the right of the television, and measured out the same distance. He then knelt in front of the wall and studied it for a few minutes.

"Well?" Belle finally demanded.

Rosco looked at Conner and said, "I saw something like this back in Newcastle. It was actually in a mansion that had belonged to a nineteenth-century sea captain, but the principal was the same . . . Do you have a wire coat hanger, or an ice pick?"

Conner nearly tripped over himself as he darted into the other room.

"What is it?" Belle asked.

"You'll see."

Conner returned with a coat hanger, and Rosco bent the hook end out straight. "The way this system works," he explained, "is by counterbalance—something like the lead weights in old window frames. You know, the type attached to a cord within the sash, that makes opening and closing the windows easier. We have them in our house, Belle . . . Anyway, in this case the weighted material sits on a small shelf inside the wall . . ." Rosco pointed the tip of the hanger toward a tiny hole hidden below the bamboo molding on the wall. "I'm not surprised no one has ever noticed this opening . . . Well, that's the whole idea, right? It's supposed to be a secret . . ."

Rosco pushed the end of the hanger through the hole, forcing an unseen object to drop from an interior shelf. There was a muffled clunk as a hidden panel slowly lifted. *"Voilà!"* Rosco pulled a small leather satchel from behind the wall, handed it to Conner, and stood. "When you slide that panel down again, the weight will automatically reseat itself on a shelf. It's a simple, but very effective, device."

They walked back to the table, and Jolly Roger dumped the contents of the satchel onto its surface. There were six or seven unusually shaped pieces of coral, a dozen shards of colored glass worn to a frosty finish from months of tumbling in the waves, a near perfect scallop shell, a small antique medicine bottle, one pearl, a shark's tooth, a corroded button, five gold coins tinged a discouraging moldy blue, a savings account passbook, and three thumbnail-sized veined and jagged green stones that could have been uncut emeralds—or perhaps just glass.

Conner opened the passbook. "It's not even his. It's from a bank in Oklahoma. Some tourist must have lost it on the beach. The last entry was thirty years ago when the account was closed out."

"Well, the coins may be worth something," Belle offered. "The emeralds, too, although . . ." She picked one up, and examined it with growing skepticism. "That is, if they're not—"

"Glass . . . which they most probably are," Conner said. He sat back in his chair.

"And the doubloons?" Rosco asked.

Conner shook his head. "They look like brass reproductions to me. And not very good ones."

The three remained motionless, staring at the dismal pile, then Jolly Roger Conner started to laugh. The sound grew in strength and amusement, an infectious, happy noise that boomed out into the darkening night. Finally, he gathered up Bonnet's "treasure" and, with great ceremony, returned it to its hiding place. "Digger left his 'loot' to me for safekeeping," he stated, "and with me it will stay—as will every single one of his very tall tales." Conner glanced up at the bungalow's ceiling. "Shiver me timbers, the old coot must be smiling now."

Jimmy Bungs hopped from Belle's shoulder onto Conner's. "Bottoms up, maties!" he cooed.

The Mystery of
Wordsworth House

ELLE Graham's dark brown fleece hat stopped just above her eyes; her red scarf stopped just below, leaving her quick and observant gray eyes the sole features exposed in an otherwise winter-muffled face and body. A bulky down jacket, long chocolate-colored wool skirt, tall snow boots, and waterproof mittens completed her wardrobe, giving her the air of a desperado headed for the Yukon Territory rather than a woman who made her living manipulating words.

"You look like a Santa's helper gone bad," her husband, Rosco, chuckled as they moved through the crowds exiting the *Champs de Mars* metro stop in Montreal, "an elf bound and determined to *rob* the sleigh rather than stuff it with goodies for little kids."

Beneath her layers of concealing warmth, her shoulders wiggled once in mirth as she mumbled a reply.

Rosco bent down toward her. "What'd you say?"

She pulled the scarf away from her nose and lips. "I said, 'Thieves don't wear red.' "

"It's not really the color I was thinking of . . . It's the you-can-only-see-my-eyes thing you've got going—"

"But it's so cold!"

"Canada's supposed to be warm? In winter? I don't think so."

"It's colder than Newcastle."

Rosco grinned. "Interesting observation . . . Maybe that's because we're further north and further from the coast. The last time I looked at an atlas, Massachusetts was—"

"Smart aleck." Belle chortled, then replaced the red scarf over her mouth. Most of her next words were lost, although Rosco heard what sounded like restaurant menu items— ". . . cheese fondue . . . crepes . . . crème brûlée . . . !"—as they passed numerous small bistros, and Belle tallied their offerings. For a person whose single culinary achievement was a plate of devilled eggs, she was exceedingly fond of food—especially the fattening variety.

By now, they were maneuvering their way across a narrow and snow-steeped sidewalk in the heart of Montreal's old city, the *vieux port.* Each carried an overstuffed overnight bag for their weekend getaway. The bags had grown heavier since detraining at the *Gare Centrale,* then jumping on the *metro* to finally traverse the small lanes that led to the wide and ice-caked Saint Lawrence River.

"Brrrr," Belle muttered.

"I take it that means you'll be cold enough tonight to require a lot of cuddling . . . flannel nightie or no."

"Head-to-foot cuddling . . ." came the chilly words. ". . . flannel nightie, *wool socks* or no." She reached out a mittened hand, took Rosco's gloved one, looked up, and again tugged her scarf loose. "Here we are—just like the directions said. Wordsworth House . . ." She cocked her head. "It looks identical to the photo in the brochure, except for the flowers in the window boxes, and the striped awnings—"

"Which may have something to do with the subzero temperature—"

"Wise guy," Belle said, but she was smiling. "What a romantic hideaway."

They paused beneath the placard announcing the bed and breakfast—WORDSWORTH HOUSE. Were it not for that single and discrete sign swinging above the sidewalk, the building might have been easily mistaken for what it once was: a private home. Lace curtains hung in each window, allowing the golden, interior light to spread outward into the snowy street; vases of magenta and yellow Persian lilies stood on polished wood tables set before entry-level windows deeply recessed within the gray stone blocks of the facade. The picture created was both welcoming and formal: an old stone house built to retain the warmth of fireplaces and cooking stoves, built to attest to a certain affluence and place in the city's long history, built, quite obviously, with pride.

"Perfect," Belle sighed.

"Except for the cold," Rosco rejoined.

"Which is precisely why we're going inside."

As they entered, the antique wood floorboards creaked in sudden discord and a bell jangled loudly, announcing the arrival of new guests, while a compact young woman appeared, hurrying down the two steps that led to the foyer. As she walked, she rubbed her hands on an apron dusted with flour. "Tomorrow morning's bread—I hope . . . Welcome, or as we say in *Montréal's Vieux Port—Bienvenue*. I'm Helene Armée. I'm your host." She gave a laugh that was as brisk and energetic as she. Like her gestures and her gait, her congenial air had a pragmatic efficiency. Helene was clearly not a person to waste time. "No, I didn't invent the name to suit my career."

In response to Rosco and Belle's perplexed glances, she added a pleasant: "*Armée* in French means a military army— or a crowd, a host of people. I am the other kind of host." Helene glanced at a guest register lying open on a writing desk at the foot of the stairs. "And you must be Belle Graham and Rosco Polycrates . . . I am pronouncing the name 'Polycrates' correctly?" Helene gave the surname its appropriate four syllables. "Greek, I think, yes?"

"Greek-American," Rosco answered.

"You are a mixture—like me. Like many of us here in Canada. Like our language here in the city. French and English on our street signs, in all our shops and restaurants. You can order in both languages; the waiters and waitresses respond in kind." Supporting that statement, Helene's accent commingled France and Great Britain; her clothes also reflected a dual heritage: a chic French skirt, a cableknit cardigan in Scottish heather tones, dark brown hair cut in feathery, Parisian bangs. "I've put you on the third floor in the front if that's acceptable. From your windows you have a view of the harbor. It's very pretty at night, especially now with the Festival of Lights on exhibit, and spotlights on the waterfront."

"Festival of Lights?" Rosco asked.

"Festival Montréal en Lumiere . . . It's quite a show, or shows, I should say. There are venues all over the city, though the principal attractions are at the *Place des Arts*— that's where our performing arts center is located."

Helene Armée led the way upstairs. The steps seemed to grumble with each footfall. *"Une vieille maison,"* she explained in French. "An old house. It was unoccupied for many years. I think it resents the return of human habitation." She made a face of mock indignation. "I do daily battle with the building."

"You bought the property in order to turn it into a B and B?" Rosco queried. He was a person keen on asking questions—a useful attribute for an ex-cop turned private investigator, or a curse, depending on how one might view it.

"No," Helene replied with some asperity. "Wordsworth House originally belonged to my great-great-grandfather. It was my grandfather who supplied the name."

"Then your ancestors were English?" Belle asked as they climbed a second set of stairs.

"Not that branch of the family, no."

In the softly lit corridor, Belle smiled. "Your grandfather must have been a lover of poetry. William Wordsworth was a romantic—"

"The name is a play on words. The surname 'Verbeux' would be translated as *verbose* in English. As to his fondness of *poésie*—poems, I'm afraid I have no answer." With that,

Helene opened a guest room door. "Here you are. Please do not hesitate to ask if there is anything you need . . . And now I will leave you. *A tout à l'heure.*" The door shut decisively behind her.

"WHAT do you think *that* was all about?" Belle turned to face Rosco, her bag in her hand, her coat and hat still on.

Rosco took the suitcase from her, but she didn't seem to notice. "You mean the fact that our hostess is busy and didn't choose to stay and gab about her forebear's taste in reading material?"

"No, Rosco, the fact that she obviously doesn't like her granddad—"

"Whoa . . . whoa . . . Hold on there, 'Miss Jump-to-Outrageous-Conclusions.' I didn't hear anything about liking or disliking." Rosco pulled off his coat and walked toward the armoire. "I guess you haven't warmed up yet, huh?"

"What do you mean?"

"You've still got your hat and coat on."

Belle sighed with the impatient sound of someone who has weightier issues at hand, then yanked off her outer garments, creating a field of static electricity that caused her fine, blond hair to rise straight up in the air. "Helene's tone positively reverberated with anger."

"Huh. I thought the way she said '*A tout à l'heure*' was kinda cute. Belle, I'll bet our hostess simply has a lot on her plate . . . As she indicated, this is a new establishment . . ." Rosco looked at his wife, unmoving in the middle of the room. Except for the strands of hair that continued pointing ceilingward, her entire being was obviously focused on a single thought. He shook his head and smiled.

"I take it your determined brain has already begun inventing family tragedies our host is unwilling to address . . . grandfather disappearing up in the Alaskan oilfields or down the darkest Amazon . . . alligators, headhunters—"

"Are there headhunters in the Amazon basin? I didn't think of that!" Belle's eyes were thoughtful.

"I take it that means you're buying the 'lost in the jungle' scenario? As opposed to the 'ravenous polar bears in the Arctic' possibility." Rosco laughed, and began unpacking. "Which side of the bed do you want?"

"Rosco! Aren't you even curious?"

"My middle name."

"Well?"

"I didn't come up here with my all-time favorite woman to start creating mysteries where none exist."

Belle, in true form, wasn't listening; instead, she was walking toward the window to gaze at the street below. "But you could tell Helene was upset, couldn't you? Old gramps was not a person she wanted to discuss."

"I don't want to discuss him, either—"

"Must have been another woman in his life—"

"Belle!"

But Belle Graham, on a roll, wasn't easily dissuaded. "Although, that's strange in itself . . . Two generations removed, and the anger and hurt remain palpable . . . You would think . . . hmmm . . ."

"What do you see out there?"

Belle turned back to Rosco. "What do——?"

"You see through the window? I.e.: How's the view?"

"The view?"

Rosco sighed. The sound was indulgent. "The view for our romantic weekend."

"Oh!" Belle spun around. "Very nice . . . Antique buildings with peaked slate roofs, icicles, smoke from chimneys . . . lots and lots of snow . . . the river completely frozen——at least the section we can see."

Rosco moved close to her and wrapped her in his arms. "A nice afternoon to stay indoors——"

Belle leaned her head against her husband's shoulder. "I can't help but wonder who he was."

"Who?"

"Helene's grandfather. Mr. Verbose."

"Did anyone ever tell you you've got a one-track mind?"

"It takes one to know one——watch where you put those mitts of yours, buddy, they're like ice."

"MAXIME Verbeux died when Helene and I were little. We never met him, however." It was Helene's first cousin, Pamela Gravers, who answered Belle's question as the three sat sipping hot cocoa near the fireplace in Wordsworth House's sitting room. Where Helene was short and precise, a devotée to detail, Pamela was lanky and tall, given to large and often incomplete gestures, and quirky, homemade garb. She was a conceptual artist based in Toronto; her visit to her cousin's B and B coincided with the *Festival Montréal en Lumiere,* where she was displaying her newest work: *Letters From Our*

Past—a celebration of the city's bilingual heritage.

As she spoke, Pamela munched distractedly on a super-chunk chocolate cookie, crumbs spilling down a handknit citron yellow pullover decorated with vivid geometrical designs in turquoise and flamingo pink. "Oops," she said, spotting the crumbs. She brushed them to the floor, then immediately regretted the action. "I keep forgetting I'm not at home. Helene's going to have my hide. She's a ferocious neatnik." A salt-stained, booted toe scuffed at the crumbs, brushing them under the chair's skirt, then she glanced at Belle and Rosco in guilty appeal. "Don't tell . . ."

"How does your installation work?" Rosco asked in a change of subject. *"Letters From Our Past?"*

"Oh! But you have to go see it!" Pamela's hand made a wide arc in the air, nearly decapitating a table lamp. The shade rocked ominously; the base teetered. Rosco reached out steadying fingers while Pamela grimaced:

"I'm going to break something, for sure. I just know it! My studio in Toronto is designed for work—not show." She grabbed another cookie, and her sweater's voluminous sleeve snagged against the plate. This time it was Belle who saved the day, retrieving sweets and china before they crashed to the floor.

Pamela produced a self-deprecating sigh, leaned forward, and continued with an impassioned and excited: "There are some wonderful installations this year . . . a modified wind tunnel with voices whose speech is tantalizingly unintelligible and enigmatic . . . a mirror-like facade that projects your image—vastly distorted—across the snow as if you'd turned into a weird extraterrestrial shadow—"

"And they're all outside?" Belle began.

"Of course! It's a matter of space, of playing with and utilizing space, of light and darkness; of experimentation—"

"But it's cold," Belle murmured.

Pamela looked at her quizzically.

"We've been discussing the 'winter in Canada' weather phenomenon," Rosco chortled.

" 'Phenomenon'?" was Pamela's perplexed response.

"The fact that it's colder up here than down near Boston, or Newcastle, which is where we live."

Pamela stared at Rosco and then at Belle. A frown of confusion crossed her brow; and Rosco realized how similar these two women were in their complete concentration on a single topic. "Unusual atmospheric conditions would be balmy breezes coming off the Saint Lawrence . . . but then the ice-skaters down at the pavilion, the *Pavillon,* would sink."

Belle shivered; Pamela Gravers laughed, then reached for another chocolate-chunk cookie. "If you're worried about being chilly, you won't be. There are bonfires to stand near, food stalls either within tents or under the stars, *en plein air,* as they say . . . and jugglers, mimes, stilt walkers . . . marsh-mallows to roast—"

"Marshmallows?" Belle said, perking up.

"You think summer picnics in the States can lay exclusive claim to marshmallows? Anyway, I'd really like you to see my installation . . . As a person whose career involves let-ters—"

"You haven't created a crossword puzzle in the snow, have you?" Belle asked.

Pamela's expression was difficult to interpret. For a moment, it seemed as though she were trying to invent a lie in response to Belle's innocent query. Then the worried behavior vanished, and her hands began moving the air as though recreating her artwork in space. "I've buried battery-powered theatre-type lamps in the snow . . . well, not completely buried, but enough so that only the round lamp face shows. And they're designed to burn cool, or else the snow would melt too quickly . . . Anyway, each face reveals the mark of a letter: a black 'A' formed by the white light around it, and so forth . . . With the help of my wizard techno-advisor and aide, Jean-Claude, I'm able to change letters continually, so my 'message,' if you will, is constantly being altered and amended——"

"Illuminated words," Belle interjected as Helene marched with customary alacrity into the room.

"What are you three talking about?" Her brow was creased in a peculiarly cross and anxious line.

"My installation piece. That's the only thing we were discussing." In a defensive gesture, Pamela Gravers slumped slightly in her chair.

"Ah, I see . . . I thought . . . Never mind."

A silence ensued. Belle could sense tension between the cousins. It was broken—or rather, avoided—when Pamela gulped an apologetic:

"I'm afraid I dropped some cookie crumbs . . . If you've got a whisk broom——"

"What are a few crumbs here and there?" Helene's tone was harsh. In an atypical gesture, the hostess of Wordsworth

House sighed while her shoulders sagged. "Let the mice eat them."

"Helene! You'd have a fit if a mouse even ventured inside this establishment."

Helene shrugged. *"N'import."*

"I'll clean up—"

"It's not important, I tell you!"

The phone rang at that moment, interrupting the awkward exchange. As their hostess hurried away, Belle and Rosco glanced at each other while Pamela stared glumly at the floor. "It's not easy, this hotelier business," she said. "As financially risky as being an artist. Maybe more so. At least, I don't have the kind of mortgage Helene has—or her overhead."

"But if this was your grandfather's home, didn't Helene inherit it?" Belle began.

"Is that what she told you?" Pamela's wary frown now mirrored that of her cousin.

"Well, no, I just assumed . . . your grandfather's house . . . 'And his grandfather's before him.' Those were Helene's words."

Pamela folded her arms across her chest. "Inherit . . ." she finally muttered, then sat straighter in her chair as her voice grew in strength and resolution. "I don't think a meaner individual than Maxime Verbeux ever existed! His two daughters—our moms—still haven't gotten over his unkindness . . . betrayal, really. Yes, they inherited this building, or rather, all four of us did. But that was the extent of his largesse. And he was a wealthy man. A very wealthy man."

Neither Belle nor Rosco spoke, and Pamela continued in the same perturbed and angry tone. "When he died, everything he owned—everything except this property—went to his second wife and her two sons from a previous marriage. Maxime was an art connoisseur. He possessed a world-famous collection of medieval manuscripts among other valuable pieces . . . but he bequeathed nothing to his natural children. Nothing except this house, which by then had become a complete wreck and was ready to be torn down. It was Helene's idea to renovate it and turn it into a commercial venture—to try to salvage something from our joint histories."

"Isn't that difficult for your two mothers?"

"They didn't grow up here, so the building has no memories—other than its unfortunate association to a father who deserted them." Pamela paused. "I guess when you mentioned the word 'illuminated' in connection with my installation piece, it triggered an unpleasant connection to old Maxime's medieval manuscripts." She shook her head. "Not that either Helene or I or our mothers aren't proud to be earning our own way, or that we believe the world owes us a living . . . It's just that . . . well, Maxime had so much . . . And it just ended up with people who aren't related to the family at all." Pamela gazed at the ceiling. "But more than the things, more than the money, what truly vanished was love."

Belle didn't respond for a long moment. Neither did Rosco. The three sat while the fire's cheery blaze threw warm and welcoming shadows across the room. However, none of the room's inhabitants drew much comfort from the sight.

At length, Pamela continued. "Our grandfather's peculiar decision left Helene's mom, and mine, wondering if perhaps their father *never* cared for them . . . or whether their memories of a happy childhood were real or honest—even asking themselves if their father might have actually *disliked* them—"

"But surely that wasn't the case?" Belle interjected.

"Who knows? Helene and I are a generation removed, but the pain inflicted on our mothers was genuine."

"How can you turn your back on your kids?" Rosco asked although his question was directed at the air. "My dad did everything in his power to ensure his offspring got a better chance than he. He went without many things to provide for us. My mother, too. It was all about making sure the next generation had more than he did."

"That's because your family is still closely tied to your European roots." Belle frowned in thought. "But it happens, Rosco. You read about situations like this more often than you'd like—wealthy families being purposely hurtful to one another . . . If you don't mind my asking, Pamela, what became of your grandfather's art collection?"

"Sold. Lock, stock, and barrel. Maxime's second wife and her sons made a sizable profit . . . Needless to say, the four stepsiblings don't communicate."

"It's a sad story." Belle shook her head in sympathy. "I guess it's not possible that we're looking at a generational custom . . . a holdover from the age when men held all the power, and women were considered chattel?"

"Chattel?" Pamela Gravers forced a wan smile. "There's an old-fashioned term."

Rosco also tried for a lighter tone. "My wife is fond of archaic phrases. It's in her blood."

"Whether or not that's the case, Belle, it doesn't alter the fact that old Maxime Verbeux disowned his daughters."

"No, it doesn't."

"But as I said: The past is the past. And perhaps Helene and I and our mothers are better off. Maybe I wouldn't be an artist if I had a cushy nest egg." Pamela attempted a plucky smile. "I wonder if the word 'chattel' bears any connection to the French *châtelaine,* the mistress of a medieval castle, a *château,* a lady whose power was certainly negligible . . ."

"I believe 'chattel' shares lexical roots with 'cattle,' " was Belle's response.

"Too bad. I was envisioning word associations between *châtelaine* and *châtiment*—'chastisement,' in English. I was beginning to think it might serve as inspiration for another installation piece."

Belle and Rosco raised their eyebrows.

"Too racy, I guess," Pamela admitted. "I'll save it for Paris." Then her momentary mood of levity disappeared. "Don't let Helene know I told you any of this. As you can see, she's sensitive when it comes to the subject of Maxime Verbeux."

"Maybe she needs to set up shop in another building," Belle offered.

"That's what her mom keeps saying, and you can imagine how successful *that* suggestion is. Helene's stubborn, and she'd definitely not about to adhere to *parental advice.* She won't even change the house's name although it's a constant reminder of mean Maxime."

"Wordsworth House brought us here," Belle said. "I liked the allusion even before we saw the brochure. Poems and words. Two of my favorite things."

"Les poemes et les paroles," Pamela translated, then she put her head to one side in thought. "I wonder what connection there is between the French for 'word' and a prison parolee?"

"Actually, I know the answer to that," Rosco said; both women looked at him in surprise. "A 'parol' was the watchword or password supplied to a guard or sentry during the days before electronic surveillance systems, etc. It has both law enforcement and military connotations . . . But I never knew our English 'word' translates to *parole.*"

"A prisoner of words," Belle mused.

AFTER Pamela Graver's description of her artwork, nothing would have kept Belle from experiencing it firsthand. She and Rosco made their way to the *Place des Arts,* asking directions along the way, none of which turned out to be necessary as the night sky above the festival site was nearly as bright as day. Plumes of crystallized vapor shot high into air that bounced with search lights, laser beams, and sparks and pulses of illumination as brilliant and varicolored as fireworks. Eerie and beautiful stilt-walking figures draped in ultralight robes bobbed and weaved, their long garments and masks turning violet or pale heliotrope or an incandescent silver while bonfires sent feathers of flame billowing into the cold, thin air; and fire-eaters, jugglers, and acrobats, also clad in space-age suits and mylar hats, either swallowed red-hot swords or balanced hoops and balls that changed shade in midair: purple to crimson, aquamarine to bronze, gold to saffron. Accompanying each visual spectacle was music orchestrated to reflect and enhance the individual performance.

"Wow . . ." Belle stared, her concealing scarf forgotten, her hat pushed high on her brow. "This is like being in the middle of some otherworldly circus. It's as if we've left planet Earth." A juggler's hoop, rimmed with fire, passed above her head. Another and another followed. There were shrieks and "oohs" and "aahs" on every side. Then a trio of acrobats mounted unicycles that appeared built entirely of glowing neon tubing. Bathed in an extraterrestrial glow, the machines seemed to dance with one another.

"Fantastic," Rosco echoed. "Stuff like this could put LSD out of business."

The couple wandered among the milling crowd, pausing to warm themselves beside the bonfires, roasting marshmallows, stepping inside one of the dining tents to sip a glass of wine.

"Let's find Pamela's installation," Belle said—which wasn't as easy a task as it seemed given the full-scale extravaganzas all around. They discovered the echoing wind tunnel that altered each speaker's voice until it became unrecognizable; a vast mirror that seemed to billow and blow, reconfiguring spectators' bodies and faces; and finally, on a man-made rise, letters that flashed on and off within the icy ground as if someone trapped under the earth were transmitting messages in code.

The wind picked up, scattering snow like sugar; the letters blinked on, blinked off; the meaning changed. ICI to ICY—"here" in Montréal to "cold," which it was. *LETTRES* to LETTERS . . . the French queen, *REINE,* to REIGN . . . *REGRET* to REPENT . . . *JOYEUX* to JOYFUL . . . *GEANTS* to GIANTS . . . *ESPERER* to its opposite, which was DESPAIR . . . *L'HIVER,* "winter," to SHIVER . . . *CONFONDRE* to CONFOUNDS . . . With each transformation, the speed accelerated until the words almost lost their meaning.

"This is fun," Belle said as hundreds of images flickered ever faster. Rosco agreed, then held her close:

"I hate to say this, but . . ."

Belle laughed. "You're freezing."

"Getting into our warm bed wouldn't be a bad idea."

"Party poop."

"I wasn't suggesting the party had to end."

A loud thud from the next door guest room awakened Belle. She looked toward the communal wall, realizing with dismay that old houses were just that: homes where noise traveled, where sound-proofing was unknown. "Darn," she muttered as the heavy tread of feet creaking across the floorboards and the murmur of a voice talking in rapid and urgent French continued to invade her space. She glanced at the clock. It was past 2 A.M. The revelers next door must

have just returned from their evening out. The voice grew
louder; there was another crash, and the solid thump of a
body hitting a piece of furniture.

"Oh darn!" Belle said. She pulled the covers over her ears.
Rosco remained deep in dreamland.

"YOU slept well, I hope?" It was Helene who spoke as she
poured coffee for Rosco and Belle. The room adjacent to a
narrow but efficient kitchen was pleasantly bright with crisp
white tablecloths covering each round table and potted
plants lining a long window ledge. The smell of cinnamon
and sautéed mushrooms perfumed the air. The sound of
something fattening sizzling in a frying pan made the morning quite perfect.

"Not exactly . . ." Belle began but their host had already
moved toward another table, repeating the identical query.
Belle looked at Rosco. "I guess our neighbors won't be down
for quite a while."

"Neighbors?" Pamela asked. She was seating herself at an
adjacent table.

"The folks next door to us," Rosco explained. "They must
have been partying late. Belle heard them come in. I
didn't . . . but then, I didn't hear much of anything."

Pamela was about to reply, but her cousin passed by, a
censorious glance indicating that family members were supposed to help rather than expect to be waited on. "I've done
it again," Pamela said. She rose but, moving between the
closely packed furniture, managed to pull the tablecloth

with her. Belle lunged for it. "A bull in a china shop," Pamela admitted.

"We really enjoyed seeing your installation last night," Belle said in response. "Especially toward the end of the exhibit: *COURAGE* to the English COURAGE, *COUR* to CORE, *MELANCOLIE* to MELANCHOLY, *COUPABLE* to CULPABLE; and the speed with which the changes occurred—"

"Speed?" Pamela demanded. "CULPABLE? MELAN-CHOLY? . . . But my intention was for a reasonable and thought-provoking pace . . . and those words weren't part of the design . . . Hmmm, maybe Jean-Claude is adding his own—"

"Pamela!"

"I'll be back. Something tells me your omelettes may be done."

SUNLIGHT glinted over every inch of road and sidewalk, dazzling the eye and making the day summer-bright. Belle leaned close to Rosco as they strolled through the old city, pressing against him not because she was cold but because she was extraordinarily happy. Happy to be alive, happy to be with the person she most loved in the world, and happy to know that her love and admiration were returned. The sorrowful tale of a man who had disowned his children hung heavily on her heart, making her give abundant thanks for all the blessings she knew had been bestowed upon her.

"We're lucky people, aren't we, Rosco?"

"I know I am."

"I am, too. Lucky to have you, friends, work I enjoy, a wonderful home—"

"A great dog."

Belle regarded her husband. "Wouldn't you say it was the other way around?"

"What do you mean?"

"That Kit owns us rather than vice versa?"

"She is a little spoiled . . ."

"A little!" Belle laughed. "In case you'd forgotten, you and I sleep in what we now refer to as 'Kit's bed.' "

"Well, where else would you want her to sack out?"

"That's *not* my point." Belle grinned, then turned to admire the scene. "What an absolutely gorgeous day! Let's walk down to the river. If we can't take a boat trip to see the sights, we can at least admire the ice-covered harbor on foot."

They wandered along the promenade that lined the waterfront, crossing the frozen river to explore a park that in summer was a glowing, emerald green and that was now transformed into an enormous skating rink. Children, couples, old, young: everyone was zooming expertly along, gliding gleefully through the air. "What a nice, old-fashioned pastime," Belle observed. "I imagine it's been the city folk's recreation since the town began."

"You mean since Jacques Cartier first admired the scenery from atop Royal Mountain—*Mont Réal*—in 1535?"

"In 1535! How did you know that?"

"Looked it up . . . The view extends over sixty miles. The 'royal' refers to King Francis the First—François the First—of France. And those famous rapids were named Lachine because Cartier thought that possibly the sea route to China lay just beyond them—*La Chine.*"

Belle laughed and shook her head. "Any other historical tidbits you'd like to trot out? Or are you just going to wait and drop them in casual conversation?"

"In 1657, a French nun—now saint—one Marguerite Bourgeoys, established the Bonsecours church in an area that was then outside the city's walls. She was Montreal's first school teacher. The first nurse was Jeanne Mance, who arrived in 1642."

"In 1642," Belle echoed. "Imagine journeying all the way from France back then . . ." She let her eyes roam up toward the center of the old city and a wide and handsome square rimmed with stately eighteenth-century buildings. "Imagine when this was nothing but forest, nothing but endless trees, wild animals, and native peoples who didn't want you to stay . . . I couldn't have braved it, that's for sure. I like my creature comforts too much."

"Are you insinuating it might be time for a cup of cocoa and a chocolate-filled pastry?"

"We did eat all of two hours ago." Belle chuckled as she linked her arm through Rosco's, then her expression grew pensive. "Perhaps the Europeans who first settled in this place needed to be so tough and hard that they were almost inhuman . . . Marguerite, Jeanne, Cartier, Champlain: they must have had iron constitutions and wills to match. And perhaps that emotional legacy is what Helene and Pamela and their mothers are dealing with right now."

Rosco nodded his head, then answered with a gentle: "Are you ready to eat?"

"When am I not ready?"

THE day was so full of sightseeing, so full of *food* and the invigorating air of winter, that Belle and Rosco were sound asleep long before the celebratory city rolled up its sidewalks. But again, Belle was awakened by their noisy neighbors' late return as they banged into furniture, gabbing loudly enough for the sound to penetrate the walls but not enough to be understood. Belle almost wished she could listen in. Eavesdropping on a private conversation would have given her a malicious pleasure that she felt was wholly justified under the circumstances. Instead, she decided to take action and protest the thoughtless behavior. She slipped out of bed without disturbing Rosco—who again lay unmoving and unconcerned—pulled on her robe, marched into the hall, and was about to knock on the adjoining door when the noise suddenly subsided.

"Hummmph," she groused, then returned to bed, but her sleeping thoughts were bombarded by an odd assortment of folk: the rough-and-ready fur traders who had originally established Montreal's wealth, the teachers, the statesmen, the priests and nuns who had struggled to create a cosmopolitan city on the banks of a vast and dangerous river, the Huron and Iroquois who had called this earth their home. All these people, flitting in and out of her dreams, existed not against the backdrop of a vibrant, modern metropolis but against a landscape of black-hearted forest and bone-breaking cold.

BELLE complained to Helene the next morning about their neighbors' heedlessness. This time the hostess of Wordsworth House put down the coffeepot, responding with a decisive: "We will talk after breakfast, yes?"

True to her word, Helene conducted them into her office an hour later. Pamela was already there standing beside a small window that faced the rear alley. The cousins exchanged glances, then Pamela waved a dismissive hand:

"A ghost isn't a problem unless you make it one, Helene."

"But disturbing people—"

"Hold on," interrupted Rosco. "Something must have gotten lost in translation. We're talking about noisy *guests,* not ghosts."

"One and the same around here," Pamela replied airily. Helene glowered at her, but Pamela paid no heed. "The room next to yours isn't occupied."

"But—" Belle began to say.

Pamela stopped her with: "And you're not the first visitor to complain of hearing noises in the night—or to infer that late-night revelers are the cause. Helene and I have discussed the situation before. Obviously, we're of two different minds. I say: Use the fact; enjoy it; capitalize on it. But Helene feels that acknowledging our supernatural chum might scare away potential customers: i.e., her guests like discovering Montreal's history, but don't want to delve into the messier details." Pamela shrugged her shoulders. "Personally, I envy you. In all the times I've visited, I've never heard a thing. If it happens again tonight, I'd love it if you'd wake me."

"This is serious, Pamela," her cousin argued.

"No, it's not, Helene. Old houses are *supposed* to be haunted. You should advertise the fact, not try to hide it . . . the true *vieux Montréal* . . . After all, *Place des Armes* was where one of the bloodiest battles was fought between the settlers and Iroquois, and nearby Saint Paul Street was no more than a dirt track leading off into some exceedingly inhospitable woods. Who knows what good or ill occurred in this vicinity—"

"The Saint Paul's that fronts the Bonsecours market?" Belle interrupted.

"And Marguerite Bourgeoys's church," was Pamela's easy reply.

"Oh!" Belle's eyes were wide. Rosco could see the wheels spinning inside her brain; for someone as amiable as she, Belle had a fascination with the lugubrious and grim. "When we were visiting the archaeology museum yesterday, we learned that Iroquois had attacked and raided the original fortifications near there."

"That's correct. The city didn't have a peaceable birth. Not by a long shot . . . And as if it weren't difficult enough carving a town out of wilderness, there were the French and Indian Wars in the 1750s when England attempted to capture the wealthy colony of New France, and the two forces' generals—the British Wolfe and French Montcalm—were mortally wounded . . . then the American Revolution with Ethan Allen and his Green Mountain Boys imprisoned in the fort here . . . Your apparition could be from any era: a soldier, a fur trader, an Iroquois chief—"

"Or a nun from the seventeenth century," Belle interjected.

Pamela nodded in agreement, but Helene remained staunch in her insistence that the purported ghost had the potential of being a serious detriment to business. "You wouldn't be so free and easy discussing metaphysical doings if it was affecting *your* work."

This accusation had a peculiar effect. Pamela's mouth tightened into a meditative and not altogether happy line. "Something *is* playing poltergeist with it," she admitted at length, and her expression grew so grave no one interrupted. "Belle said she and Rosco saw *MELANCOLIE* change into MELANCHOLY, *COUPABLE* morph into CULPABLE . . . none of which were in the original *mots croisés,* and Jean-Claude maintains he had nothing to do with it."

"*Mots croisés?*" Belle asked.

"Crossword . . ." Pamela's shoulders hunched in guilty confession. "It was a puzzle I used as inspiration—"

Helene gasped. "Not Verbeux! What if our mothers learned you were paying him homage with your *Letters From Our Past?*"

"But I'm not honoring him . . . I just liked the notion of black words against a snow white ground. The puzzle inspired me. I only borrowed a few of his—"

Helene's eyes narrowed; her nose grew pinched and angry. "Well, it serves you right if the machinery goes on the fritz, and spoils your fun!"

"You're being silly, Helene—"

"No, I'm not! The man didn't care two *centimes* for his children! He doesn't deserve even this much consideration—"

"But I haven't—"

"Could I interrupt for a moment?" Belle asked. The two warring parties spun toward her: Pamela in defensive sorrow, Helene in self-righteous indignation. "Your grandfather constructed crossword puzzles?"

"Heaps," was Pamela's ready reply.

"And we threw away every one of them as soon as we found them," Helene spat out.

"But I take it one was saved?" Rosco interjected.

Pamela nodded slowly. "Despite everything Maxim Verbeux did—or failed to do—the utter extinction of his memory seemed so terribly sad. There was nothing left to connect us with the old man . . . no letters or photographs . . . just a boxful of *mots croisés* hidden in a closet upstairs. I had to rescue one."

"And you're certain it was your grandfather's creation?" Belle asked.

"He signed it, and also entitled it *Poetic Justice* . . . Given the name of the house, I simply couldn't consign it to the trash."

Helene snorted in wrathful exasperation, but Belle ignored their hostess. "I'd like to see it if I might."

"It's in my room."

Helene sighed afresh, then affixed a tight smile for her guests' behalf. "If you will excuse me, I have *work* to attend to."

LEADING the way to her room, Pamela gave a brief, embarrassed laugh as she attempted to dismiss her cousin's censure. "Helene doesn't view what I do as *work,* I'm afraid."

Belle smiled in sympathy. "I hear the same type of criticism all the time." Then she changed the subject. "Tell me about this poltergeist notion again."

"Yesterday, when you shared your reaction to my installation piece, I realized you'd seen four words I hadn't built into the design. You also mentioned how hectic and hurried the changes became. So I looked at the video . . . a tape is automatically made of each performance, and I was amazed at the alterations—and the speed. My technical assistant swore the device was working perfectly, so the only explanation is—"

"Ghostly intervention," Belle interjected.

"I know it seems far-fetched."

"Not if you believe *this* house is haunted, Pamela. And quite truthfully, I've experienced the phenomenon before."

Pamela blinked. "You're kidding."

"It was in an ancient home," Rosco added. "In England. Belle discovered a segment from a crossword, and assumed our hosts were playing a practical joke."

"But they weren't." Pamela's response was statement rather than query. "And when you look at Verbeux's puzzle, you'll know why I have my suspicions; it's odd to the point of seeming like poetic smoke and mirrors."

ACROSS

1. Ottawa dealmaker
4. Hoover; slang
7. Ghostly sound
10. Smoked meat
13. Gorilla; e.g.
14. Here in Montréal
15. Newt
16. Mr. Yale
17. enfin . . .
21. Metal bar
22. 35-Down quaff
23. Goofed
24. "____was in the beginning . . ."
25. A day in Dorado
26. Columbus' ship
27. Layer
28. Does without
30. Com. giant
31. enfin . . .
36. Perfect mark
37. Turncoat
38. enfin . . .
46. Tear
47. Illuminators
48. Pester
50. Mine entrance
52. Celtics' org.
53. Spy in France
54. Southern nut
56. Sumerian world of the dead
57. Phi Beta____
58. enfin . . .
61. Continent of Fr.
62. Female sheep
63. Shaker founder, Lee
64. Wee one
65. Postal abbr.
66. Min. neighbor
67. Fishing gear
68. Switch positions

DOWN

1. Outcast
2. Liner bailiwick
3. Warm outerwear
4. Hanoi native
5. Perform
6. Provence pipers?
7. Down under
8. Switch position
9. Siouan
10. Ruler of France, 1589–1610
11. Pasta request
12. Accounting error
18. Decay
19. Pindar; e.g.
20. Café pot
28. Last
29. Slaves
32. List ender
33. N.J. neighbor
34. Malay gibbon
35. Montréal summer
38. Furrier
39. Go on the lam
40. Connoisseur
41. 1863 Unions?
42. Inspire
43. Disciplined
44. Sits upright
45. Whaler's lance

🌴 *Poetic Justice* 🌴

49. "____ in the Earth," Rölvaag novel
51. Salt
53. Owns
55. Compass pts.
57. ____Peninsula, N.W.T
59. The Great War; abbr.
60. Heading for 26-Across

OH, I see!" Belle said as she perched on Pamela's bed, her concentration wholly on Maxime Verbeux's crossword. She looked up at the artist after several long and studious moments. "But what on earth does the message mean? I assume it is a message . . . a sort of Haiku . . . here, beginning at 17-Across?"

"You mean the four *enfin* clues?"

"Yes . . . How do you translate *enfin*?"

" 'Finally,' " Pamela said. "It can also mean, 'At last!' "

Then she recited her grandfather's peculiar poem. "REGRET CONFOUNDS / AGED IS THE LEVEE / THE CLAY IS FRESH / POUR SWEETNESS ON."

Rosco winced. Pamela looked at him and shook her head.

"I know what you're thinking," she said. "A Wordsworth, he was not."

71

"Maybe something was lost in translation," Belle observed, returning her focus to the crossword.

"But that's just it. The puzzle is in English . . . Besides, our moms said their father was an excellent linguist and spoke several languages fluently. I don't believe his poem—if you will—is a mistake. On the other hand, I've never been able to make any sense of it."

"*Enfin* . . ." Belle muttered. "REGRET . . . REGRET . . . REPENT . . . That was the translation you used in your show!"

Pamela stared at her uncomprehending. "It's common usage."

Belle bounced on the bed as she stared up at Pamela. "But what if old Verbeux is 'repenting'? What if this is a message of apology? REGRET CONFOUNDS sure seems like an indication of remorse to me."

Pamela smiled sadly. "I don't know, Belle—"

"And *enfin* . . . which sounds like *enfants*—children."

"They're not completely similar—" Pamela began, but Belle, in her excitement, cut her short.

"The words are alike if you say them fast enough." Belle repeated both *enfin* and *enfants* ten times, increasing in speed until the vowels and consonants blurred. "And that's what happened at your installation. "Everything began running together—which you said hadn't been your intention at all."

"This is pretty far-fetched, Belle," Rosco interjected. "Even for you."

"Look, we're all in agreement about the ghost thing, right?"

Rosco shook his head. "Well, I didn't hear it—"

"Nothing wakes you up," Belle chortled, before returning to her hypothesis. "Okay . . . 17-Across: REGRET CONFOUNDS . . . Your grandfather is stating that he is deeply troubled by his past actions toward his *enfants,* his children . . ."

Pamela squinted in skepticism while Rosco asked a straightforward:

"AGED IS THE LEVEE?"

"I don't know. We'll get to that in a moment—"

"And the FRESH CLAY?" Pamela teased, but Belle was too all-consumed to note the tone.

"SWEETNESS," she mumbled, "SWEETNESS . . ." Then all at once she gasped. "What's 'SWEETNESS' in French?"

"*Douceur.*"

"Which sounds like *deux soeurs*—'two sisters'!"

"Well, the intonation isn't precisely—" Pamela started to protest.

"But it's close! And *Pour* in English is 'for' . . . *Pour deux soeurs.* 'For two sisters'!" She bounced higher on the bed. "And ON . . ."

By now Pamela was beginning to catch a little of Belle's enthusiasm. "*ON* in French can mean either 'one,' 'people,' or 'they'—"

"That's you!" Belle all but yipped. "You and Helene— the offspring of *les deux soeurs!*"

Rosco picked up the crossword. "So, Mr. Verbeux's two offspring—the sisters and their daughters—are supposed to find some ancient riverbank, and patch it up with new clay? That doesn't sound like much of an apology—"

"Bank," Belle almost shouted. "You're brilliant, Rosco! Old bank . . ." She stared at Pamela, whose eyes had grown enormous:

"La Vieille Banque de Montréal—"

"Where it's conceivable," Belle continued, "that a patron might use a key which in French is *clef* pronounced 'CLAY.' "

"To open a safe-deposit box?" Rosco demanded. "I admit it's an intriguing story, but . . ."

Pamela's shoulders slumped dispiritedly. "And which *Vieille Banque de Montréal?* There must be twenty branches within the city limits alone . . . Sorry, Belle. Thank you for spinning this lovely fairy tale, but I'm afraid that's all it is." She sighed. "Maybe it's simply another case of my grandfather's meanness. Give hope, and then dash it."

But Belle, once convinced, was stubbornness itself. "Let's go back to the first line of the *Poetic Justice* haiku thing . . . We must have missed something . . . REGRET . . . REPENT . . . synonyms: bewail, mourn, rue . . . *rue,* as in street! There's your clue! The bank's on—"

"Confounded Street?" Rosco demanded.

Belle gave him a temperamental glance, then turned to Pamela. "Do you have a phone book that lists the bank's branch offices? We should look for one in a place where—"

"Where everything's confused and blurred," Rosco said; then shrugged. "It's all French to me."

"Rosco!"

"I'm just trying to help—"

"No, you're not—"

74

But Pamela interrupted. "Here," she announced. "There's a bank on the *rue de Bluery.*"

Belle's mouth fell open. "Blurry . . . that's what happened to the words in your installation—"

"I still don't—" Rosco started, but Belle silenced him with an impassioned:

"The old man was probably heartsick at cutting his children out of his will. That makes sense, doesn't it? More so than simply being a self-serving old miser who disowned his true heirs . . . But maybe he couldn't change the official document, Rosco . . . Maybe his then wife or her sons had some means of preventing him from making the necessary . . ." The theory vanished as Belle began to attack a more immediate conundrum. "What we need is a FRESH *clef*—key . . . Green, do you think, Pamela? It can't mean 'new,' because your grandfather . . . ?"

Pamela shook her head, a small smile growing on her lips. "FRESH translates to *frais* . . . but *fraise* means a 'strawberry.' I found a number of odd-looking large and small keys among Maxime's puzzles. Helene tossed them out in a fit of pique when none proved serviceable, but I kept the smallest. It has a charming mark of a berry."

THE cousins, with Rosco and Belle, stood in the venerable vault of the equally venerable banking institution situated on the *rue de Bluery;* aiding them, however, was not a remnant from the city's past but a young man in a new and ultramodern suit. He looked no more than eighteen; and his clothing appeared to have just come off the rack at some impossibly hip and trendy store. "One of the old 'strawberry' keys," he mused with a lofty smile. "I didn't realize they were still in private hands." He regarded the bank of vaults, searching for the corresponding number.

"But wouldn't we—or our mothers—have been contacted when the box's lessee died?" Helene ventured.

The "boy" scowled as he drew himself and his shiny black suit up in a perfect replica of austere and wounded age. "*Madame,* we at *La Vieille Banque de Montréal* pride ourselves on our discretion. The gentleman in whose name the contract was held paid a considerable sum for a quarter of a century's worth of service and security. In fact, it is the responsibility of said *heirs* to inform *La Vieille Banque de Montréal* of a lessee's demise." He all but glowered at their naiveté and fecklessness.

"And after the contract expires?" Helene persisted.

"The contents are auctioned. No names are supplied—again, for discretion's sake; but objects such as jewelry and so forth are listed in the newspaper." He studied the card that contained Maxime Verbeux's particulars. "At the close of this calendar year, we would have drilled out the lock, and emptied the vault. We abide by strict protocol here at *La Vieille Banque.*"

"We're lucky we found this when we did, then," Pamela offered, but the "boy" merely gave her a glance that further established his superiority. "Lucky" was not a term employed in old and respected financial institutions.

Pamela said no more; neither did Helene, but they held each other's hands in anxious anticipation as the key turned in the lock. A bronze and steel door swung open to reveal a box twelve inches square and two feet in length. Normally, banking patrons would be given the courtesy of examining the contents in a private room, but the boy clearly considered the cousins too irresponsible to be left alone. He opened the box's lid in front of them.

Inside was a typed list cataloging the contents. Below were ancient books wrapped in translucent tissue. From the edges of the vellum pages shimmered gold leaf and cobalt blue, ruby red and a green as pure as fresh-mown grass: Maxime Verbeux's renowned collection of medieval manuscripts. Infirm and shaky handwriting scrawled across the top of the list. *Pour les deux soeurs.*

Letters from the past.

A Crossworder's Gift

O H yeah, you can bet your very last wooden nickel on that, pardner, there is no place, I mean *no* place, in the world like Vegas for the holidays." The bellhop, dressed in a movie-set version of a Native American Indian—war paint, feathered headdress, and all—pulled Belle and Rosco's bags from the trunk of their bright green rental car, then tossed them onto a gold-trimmed luggage cart that vaguely resembled a high-end stagecoach—*sans* horses. As he wheeled the cart into the hotel lobby, he added, "Just look at that, will you . . . Where else do you get that on Turkey Day? Where?" He was pointing to a statuesque redhead manning the concierge desk of Cactus Cal's Hotel and Casino. Since it was just the Friday following Thanksgiving, she had not yet changed from her abbreviated "Puritan" outfit into something more "Christmasy." The "Puritan" number consisted of a low-cut black dress whose full skirt was a micromini, and a bibbed apron that was even shorter at the hem and deeper at the neckline. A starched white hat that was a combination of wimple and bonnet seemed to contain more fabric than either skirt or bodice.

"Who knew those early settlers were so well . . . put together," Rosco said, "Is that scarlet 'A' on her, er, whatever, chest . . . is it a real tattoo?"

Belle narrowed her eyes into a squint that failed to cover any potential jealous streak. "We just flew in from Massachusetts," she said, addressing the bellhop with a small smile, "and the temperature at Plymouth Rock was only twenty-eight degrees this morning . . . I think your concierge would stand a good chance of freezing to death in that getup."

The bellhop chuckled. "Oh that's nothing. In a day or two Angie, that's what the 'A' stands for, will be changing into her 'Santa's Little Helper' wardrobe. I don't know how she keeps from popping out of it, I really don't."

"Hmmm," Rosco replied. "That's something to look forward to."

"Yep, the colder it gets in the East, the skimpier the outfits seem to get—go figure. Yes sirree, Bob, there's no place like Vegas for the holidays."

Belle smiled again, albeit a bit stiffly. However, despite Angie and her female cohorts' singular apparel, Belle was truly pleased to be in a locale that hadn't rushed the season. Unlike the New England shopping malls, there were no Christmas trees, no menorahs, no plastic icicles dangling from the chandeliers, no giant snowflakes, reindeer, merry little elves, or Santas anywhere to be found—not yet, at least. Here was a place that seemed to take every season according to the calendar—finish up with one before taking on the decor of another. She found it refreshing.

"So what brings you nice young folks out to Las Vegas on this sunny Friday afternoon? Business or pleasure?" the bellhop asked as he maneuvered their luggage down a long corridor toward Cactus Cal's front desk. The passage was lined with nickel slots; over half the machines had players perched anxiously before them. Both Belle and Rosco became mesmerized by the flashing lights; the whirling cartoon pictures of cherries, bananas, and plums; the chime of bells, whistles, horns, and electronic keyboard crescendos—and the shrieks of the latest winners. The couple had never seen—or heard anything like it; the bellhop was forced to repeat his question.

"You don't look like seasoned gamblers to me," he added. "You have what I call that 'starry-eyed-rookie-can't-wait-to-get-at-it' gaze. So what is it, business or pleasure?"

Simultaneously Belle said, "Business," while Rosco voiced, "Pleasure."

The bellhop laughed. "Well, whatever. Enjoy your stay. I'll get your car keys from valet parking, and have your bags transferred to your room as soon as you're finished checking in."

The desk clerk, a short, ball-shaped, middle-aged male, was decked out in a more modified "Puritan" garb than the concierge—his attire being dark trousers, a high-buttoned black jacket that rounded over his ample belly, a white jabot, and a miniature version of a Pilgrim's tall buckled hat, which he wore tilted Stetson-like on his head: twenty-first-century Nevada meets seventeenth-century England. He greeted them with a warm and friendly smile, adding a laconic "Howdy, folks" that didn't seem in keeping with the implied severity of his costume.

Rosco returned the smile and said, "We have a reservation for three nights. The name is Polycrates." He placed his credit card on the counter.

The clerk entered the name into his computer and waited for information to appear on the screen.

"Hmmm," he eventually said, "I don't seem to have anything here under that name."

"P-O-L-Y-C-R—"

"Yes, sir, I've spelled it the same as it appears on the card." He continued to stare at the screen. "Nope . . . Sorry, sir, but I—"

"The reservation should have been made by the Blue Diamond Wildlife Shelter."

"Nope . . . I don't have Blue Diamond in here either—"

Belle stepped forward. "Perhaps, you have it under my name . . . Annabella . . . Belle Graham?"

The clerk's fleshy face jerked upward. "Oh, sure . . . yes, *of course,* Miss Graham. I didn't realize . . . I mean, we've been expecting you. I'm sorry I didn't recognize you on the spot. Everyone was *so* excited to hear that you'd be staying with us for a few days. I mean, my sister and niece sure were . . . They have every one of your crossword collections. Those two just adore your puzzles."

"Thank you, that's nice to hear. And of course, this is my husband, Rosco—Mr. Polycrates."

"And he decided not to change his name when you got married? How absolutely modern!" The clerk chortled energetically at his own joke; his black hat bounced merrily. "Sorry, sir, just a little humor on my part."

Rosco nodded although his expression wasn't enthusiastic. It was a jest he'd been subjected to one too many times.

"It must be difficult being married to such a famous lady," the clerk continued blithely. "Oh, before I forget. There are some messages for you, Miss Graham." He handed her two slips of hotel stationery. One read: *Please call Karen Wise;* the other: *Stan Hollister, LVMPD.* Both had an accompanying phone number.

"The woman from the Wildlife Shelter, and Lieutenant Hollister," Belle murmured under her breath as she handed the notes to Rosco.

The desk clerk placed Rosco's credit card slip and a small booklet on the counter. "If you would be kind enough to sign here at the 'X,' Mr. Graham . . . er, *Polycrates* . . . This brochure will explain our many features here at Cactus Cal's Hotel and Casino. Naturally, all three restaurants are open twenty-four/seven, as well as the gambling tables and slots. Additionally, you'll find slot machines poolside, at the tennis courts, in the salon and barber shop, and at the end of the corridor on every floor of guest suites. Of course, the volume on the machines in the residential areas is turned off for your comfort when napping. Some guests don't appreciate the noise. What can I say? Party poops, I guess. If you need anything *special* sent to your room, just speak to Angie at the concierge desk."

"Special?" Rosco asked.

The clerk winked at him and said, "Like, reading or *viewing* materials?"

"I see."

"I've also taken the liberty of giving you a suite on the tenth floor, just down the hall from where Dr. Jazz, Mr. Dave Narone, that is, died . . . Sorry, but there aren't many secrets in Vegas, and everyone knows that's why you both are here. I thought by giving you a room on the tenth floor, it would be easier for you to *get the lay of the land,* so to speak."

"Thank you," Belle said. "Is Mr. Narone's room sealed or have you given it to other guests?"

"Oh, goodness no! The police have it locked up tighter than a rattlesnake's fist."

Rosco frowned slightly; the clerk gave him a cherubic smile. "An expression we have out here."

"I see," Rosco said again. "And since there are no secrets in Las Vegas, has the cause of Mr. Narone's death been classified yet?"

The clerk became innocence itself. "You'll have to check with Lieutenant Hollister on that point. All I can say is that Dr. Jazz will be sorely missed around this casino. Sorely missed, indeed. He was, without a doubt, the classiest *high roller* of them all. A 'whale,' as we call folks like him out here. The biggest darn thing in the whole darn sandy ocean . . . Even though his accommodations were comped, he took care of the little guy—if you know what I mean." The clerk graced Rosco with another high-wattage grin that seemed to indicate he wouldn't be averse to some palm greasing, but Rosco merely nodded, picked up the key to

Suite 1014, and handed it to the bellhop, who escorted them up to their room.

THE suite was far more lavish than any hotel room Rosco and Belle had ever stayed in. The sitting room was larger than their living room back home. It had a huge wraparound leather couch; an *entertainment unit* with DVD, VCR, CD, and tape players; and a TV screen that seemed bigger than many multiplex movie theater screens. The walls were decorated with reproduction French Impressionist paintings: Cézanne, Manet, Monet, Matisse, Corot—an upscale gang that seemed out of place in a hostelry known as Cactus Cal's. There was a marble-countered kitchen, a minibar, pile carpet so thick it felt like the densest of furs, and an expansive balcony overlooking the Las Vegas "Strip." Even though the sun had yet to set, most of the casinos were already illuminated with a full battery of electric lights that washed the desert sky in colors normally reserved for lush, tropical paradises.

Rosco tipped the bellhop, and strolled from the sitting area into the suite's bedroom. Again, everything was oversized. The bed appeared large enough to play basketball on; and there was also a hot tub that had apparently been designed to easily accommodate more than two bodies.

Rosco turned to Belle. "This was definitely made for recreational activity."

"I'll say."

He gave her a long soft kiss. "So?"

"Seems like *Angie's* put some ideas into your head."

"Angie? Angie? Who's Angie?"

"Methinks the gent doth protest too much . . . You couldn't take your eyes off her *tattoo* downstairs."

Rosco opened his mouth to object, but the sudden ringing of the telephone cut him short.

"I'll get it," Belle said. She walked to the bed stand and lifted the receiver. Rosco followed, placed his arms around her waist, and kissed the back of her neck. After a "Hello . . . Sure . . . Fine," and a "See you then," Belle replaced the receiver in the cradle. "That was Lieutenant Hollister. He was in the neighborhood; he's stopping by."

"Now? He's stopping by *now*?"

"Why not?"

"I thought we might . . . You know . . ." He glanced at the oversized bed. "Take a nap? Jet lag and all?" He looked at his watch. "Wow, it's darn near seven P.M. back East." He stretched his arms, and put on a fake yawn.

She kissed him. "I do love you, Rosco, but this is a business trip, remember?"

"Right."

They spent the next few minutes unpacking, and hadn't quite finished when they heard three hard knocks at the door.

"I see some folks don't feel the need to go through the formality of having the front desk announce them." Rosco made no attempt to cover his disapproval. He opened the door without bothering to ask who it was, or use the peephole.

Hollister was a good deal taller than Rosco, about six foot five, and wore a light tan Western-style suit with lizardskin cowboy boots. He was probably forty years old, with thick brown hair, a healthy mustache, and a deep tan that etched the contours of an angular, don't-coop-me-up, outdoorsy face. He held a wide-brimmed hat in his left hand, and extended his right to Rosco as he strode uninvited into the room. His grip was solid, intended to let the other person know just exactly whom they'd be dealing with.

"Pleased to meet you, Mr.*Pol-y-crates.*" He gave the name three syllables, coming down hard on the first and making it sound like "pole." "I realize you used to be on a police force in Massachusetts; and you may think you Easterners have cornered the market on crime, but things can get just as nasty in Vegas. You folks should be a little more cautious about opening hotel doors to strangers." He nodded perfunctorily toward Belle. "Ma'am."

Rosco cleared his throat. "Actually, back East my name gets a different reading—Pah-lick-rah-tees, stress on the *lick*. But why don't you call me Rosco."

"Not a problem."

Rosco pointed to a grouping of table and chairs. "Shall we have a seat?"

Hollister's face creased in what obviously passed as a smile. "I'd like to take you to the suite Dave Narone kept here first, Rosco. It's Number 1015."

"Sounds good."

As they walked down the hall, Rosco began second-guessing the real reason he and Belle had been placed in Suite 1014. Perhaps it was more for the lieutenant's convenience than their own?

The dead man's accommodations were the mirror image

of Belle and Rosco's. The furniture and carpeting were identical, as were the kitchen and hot tub. But there were also noticeable differences. The suite was filled with personal effects: books, magazines, knickknacks, a closet full of clothing, and photos—many of Dr. Jazz with an aging collie identified as "Trevor." There was also a funerary cremation urn with the dog's name on a brass plaque. Belle stared at the urn for a long, sad minute as she considered how much love the dead man must have felt for this obviously adored canine. Then she thought of Kit, the dog she and Rosco had left at home. Kit was still in her puppyhood, but . . . but . . . Finally, reflectively, Belle returned her attention to the job at hand. She noted genuine Southwestern landscapes in place of the reproduction artwork in the other suite, and the room's *pièce de résistance*—a white baby grand piano in one corner of the sitting area. The rooms had obviously been "home" to Dave Narone for some time. Another fact was also immediately apparent: Someone—either an intruder or the Las Vegas police—had pawed through everything.

After their tour, Belle, Rosco, and Hollister sat on the sectional couch. "I'd like y'all to bring me up to date on what's goin' on between you and Karen Wise," Hollister said in his slow, "I'm-the-man-in-charge" drawl. "Don't skip over anything you think I might already be aware of. I'll let y'all know if you're boring me."

Belle could sense, rather than see, Rosco bristle at the lieutenant's condescending attitude, so she jumped in before a battle—or even a skirmish—could begin: "You know about Dave Narone's list of words?"

"Why don't you just start from the beginning, ma'am."

This time it was Belle who experienced a twinge of irritation. She had a name—a well-known name; and she didn't expect to be treated like the "little lady" or "other half." Her gray eyes flashed, then narrowed into indignant slits, while Rosco settled into the sectional's cushions.

He'd been in Hollister's position more than once when he'd been on the Newcastle police force: attempting to extract information from one witness—or suspect—after another, while looking for inconsistencies that might steer an investigation in the right direction; and although he found it odd to be on the other side of the interrogation, he knew Hollister had a job to do.

On the other hand, Rosco didn't like being pushed around, and he liked seeing his wife in that position even less. "I understand you're with Homicide, Lieutenant? Does that mean that LVMPD is classifying Dr. Jazz's death a murder?"

Hollister took a moment to speak. Like Rosco, he also leaned back, his long legs sprawling across the couch and his boots planted in the carpeting as if stuck in stirrups hanging from a wide-backed horse. "I have to tell you . . . *Rosco,* I'm not a real fan of private detectives. Las Vegas has more of the buggers than you can shake a stick at. Most are as slippery as a forty-pound eel. Slipperier, some of 'em."

Rosco's smile was thin. "Fair enough, but I'm not from Las Vegas, and 'slippery as an eel,' as homey as it might sound, doesn't really answer my question, does it? All I want to know is if a man was murdered in this room."

"Tough guy from the East Coast, is that it?"

Rosco leaned forward. "We came here to help, Lieutenant. Think what you will." He looked at Belle. "Why don't *you* explain what we know, *Ms.* Graham."

As much as she loved her husband, Belle didn't relish the idea of becoming a tennis ball bouncing between two testosterone-laced rackets, so she stood, and walked to the back of the couch to sit on a bar stool. The men were forced to turn and face her. "Well, Lieutenant . . ." Belle pasted on a high-wattage grin intended to establish her femininity and superior brain power. "I don't imagine we know more about this situation than you, but here goes . . . On the Monday before Thanksgiving, I received a telephone call from Karen Wise of the Blue Diamond Wildlife Shelter. She told me that Dave Narone, also known as Dr. Jazz, was found dead a few days earlier—"

"Last Friday, that would have been," Rosco tossed in, and received a cold stare from Hollister.

"Karen—Ms. Wise—explained that according to Mr. Narone's will, all of his assets—stocks, bonds, and bank holdings—were to go to his nephew, Reggie daCoit . . . Does that jibe with your information?"

Belle looked at Hollister for a reply, but he remained poker-faced, saying, "Go on," without blinking or seeming to move his lips.

"The other stipulation of Narone's legacy was that the Blue Diamond Wildlife Shelter would be the beneficiary of everything found in this suite—and on his person. Which seems to me a very kind gesture. These are wonderful and evocative paintings." Belle gestured toward seven canvases, each created by an obviously talented artist. There was also a framed straight flush—ace through five of diamonds—

that hung above the wet bar, with the inscription *You're a Lucky Son-of-a-Gun.* It was signed *Gabby.*

"I would imagine these oils are quite valuable." Although Belle's comment wasn't posed as a question, she waited for a response from Hollister. Nothing was forthcoming, so she pushed ahead. "Karen Wise explained that the night before he died, Dr. Jazz had won close to three hundred thousand dollars in a high-stakes poker game. Is that correct?"

This time Hollister acquiesced, and gave Belle a brief nod of agreement.

"And no one knows where that money is now? It never appeared in his bank or casino account, and is nowhere in this suite, correct?"

"Correct."

"Which brings us to Dr. Jazz's 'list of words,' entitled *Still, Man Wasted Talent.* The list Karen faxed to me—"

"Yes, I have a copy of that document right here. As well as the word game you created and then relayed to Ms. Wise as per the deceased's stipulation." Hollister removed two folded sheets of paper from his jacket pocket and read an inscription at the top of the first, *"As my will indicates, all my liquid cash assets are bequeathed to my sole heir, my nephew, Reggie daCoit, while everything within this suite, and on my person, shall go to the Blue Diamond Wildlife Shelter in care of one Karen Wise.*

"But because my nephew has a certain unfortunate reputation, it is necessary for me to become cryptic in voicing my wishes as to the disposal of certain non-liquid assets, thus, Still, Man Wasted Talent:

"Below is a list of words. They represent a selection of out-of-

order ACROSS solutions to a crossword puzzle. It is my wish that a puzzle grid be created by one Anna Graham of Newcastle, Massachusetts in order to accommodate these answers. When said grid is complete, a message will reveal the particular arrangement of those non-liquid assets. Although it is only a puzzle, there is good reason to—fear of it, however cute."

Hollister raised his eyes from the paper. "If Dr. Jazz is talking about his recent three hundred thousand dollars in winnings with this gobbledygook, then I'm a monkey's uncle . . . But hey, little lady, you're supposed to be the puzzle pro; what did you discover?"

" 'Little lady'?" Rosco snapped. "Do you really talk like that, or is this just your 'Marshal Dillon' routine?"

Hollister was a man accustomed to having people step out of his way; Rosco's blowup not only surprised, but confounded him. "No disrespect intended" served as a cursory apology before the lieutenant resumed his authoritarian tone. "I fail to see any connection—or resolution—to the disposal of Narone's assets in this gibberish."

Belle returned to the couch. "I was asked to come to Las Vegas to find answers, Lieutenant. If you can accept the fact that this admittedly obscure and curious document serves as Narone's final wishes, maybe we can get somewhere."

Hollister regarded her. Belle could almost see his brain wrestling with two major problems. One: "Little ladies" didn't challenge police lieutenants; and Two: "Anna Graham" and her husband had been officially brought in on the case. "Shoot," Hollister eventually said.

Belle smiled; it was a triumphant rather than a conciliatory expression. "The crossword I constructed according to the deceased's instructions represents the only solution I was able to devise. As you can see"—she pointed to the puzzle Hollister was holding—"at 26-Across and 40-Across, where I would hope to find some answers, the words formed are unintelligible. If there's a message, I haven't found it." Belle paused, her face softening in concern. "We're on your side, Lieutenant. You have to believe that."

Hollister remained silent for nearly a minute. Eventually he took a large breath and exhaled slowly. "Okay, I'm going to level with you. Dave Narone had enough strychnine in his system to kill a Brahma Bull—and his last four riders. Samples were also found on a bourbon glass next to the body."

Belle frowned, then wrapped her arms around herself while Rosco responded:

"So, you're classifying this as homicide."

Belle looked around the room; her expression was troubled. "What about suicide?"

It was Rosco who answered. "Nobody commits suicide with strychnine. It's a horrendous way to die. Basically, it's rat poison."

Belle shivered and hunched her shoulders. Her eyes dropped to the floor.

"Your husband's right. Besides, Dr. Jazz was on the top of his game. He had no reason to kill himself."

"Any suspects, Lieutenant?" In an attempt to clear the air, Rosco's tone was respectful.

"I'm starting with the obvious: the two people who stand to gain from the death—your friend, our local 'wise woman,' and Narone's good-for-nothing nephew."

"What do you mean by 'our local wise woman'?" Belle

protested. "It seems to me she's doing an admirable job, rescuing animals—"

It was Rosco who interrupted what was threatening to become a very cranky broadside. His wife was swift to defend anyone or anything she felt was under attack; and Hollister's tone had been more than snide. " 'Good-for-nothing nephew'?" he asked.

"Like Narone indicated, daCoit has an 'unfortunate reputation.' He's a small-time con man . . . hails from down Phoenix way, and has been in and out of the hoosegow more times than a duck lays eggs. He drifts into Las Vegas every now and then. I imagine it was mostly to hustle some *dinero* out of his rich uncle."

"Was daCoit here at the time of the murder?"

"He claims not, but his alibi's as thin as a Mojave coyote. He maintains he was in Los Angeles at the time. We're checking it out."

"This place looks like it was inspected pretty thoroughly," Rosco said. "Was it your investigation unit . . . or was someone searching for Narone's three hundred grand?"

"My unit found the premises like this. They're a solid crew."

"Then you're assuming the perp found—and pocketed—Narone's winnings? Maybe, a sore loser scenario?"

"There's no room for sore losers when you're out there with the 'whales' . . . High-stakes players lose a quarter mil one night, win it back the next. As to my assumptions . . ." Hollister left the sentence unfinished as he escorted Belle and Rosco from Dr. Jazz's suite, and locked the door. "Right now your buddy at Blue Diamond is a prime suspect, and if that list of words proves to be important, you two are in it up to your keisters, as well . . . I don't want you two to leave Las Vegas without notifying me first, and I mean that." He strode down the hall and stepped onto the elevator.

" 'Up to our keisters'?" Rosco grumbled. "What'd we get here? The Yiddish Wyatt Earp?"

Belle cocked her head. "You shouldn't allow your masculinity to get bruised so easily."

"Masculinity? What? Bruised?From that guy? You just like him because he looks so much like Gary Cooper."

"He does look a lot like Gary Cooper, now that you mention it . . . Did you ever see *Meet John Doe?*"

"No. And I never want to see it if it's going to remind me of our upstanding Lieutenant Hollister."

"It's a good movie."

"I don't care."

They stepped across the hallway and into their own suite. Belle turned and gave Rosco a deep kiss. "I do love you, Rosco, and I'm awfully glad you don't throw around phrases like 'our wise woman.' "

"I love you too . . . But I'm never seeing *Meet John Doe,* not in a million years."

Belle laughed. "I guess we should return Karen's call. At least, let her know we've arrived." She walked to the writing desk, but the phone rang before she could reach for it.

"Speak of the devil," Rosco said.

"How do you know it's her?"

"Hey, this is Las Vegas. Want to bet on it? I'll give you two-to-one odds . . . But—if it turns out to be Angie? I'll take it in the other room."

Belle stuck her tongue out at him before picking up the receiver. It was Karen Wise, as he'd predicted. She suggested that they get together the following morning, and gave Belle directions to Blue Diamond, Nevada. It was just outside the Las Vegas sprawl, to the southwest on Route 160.

"So," Rosco said as he stepped up behind Belle, wrapped his arms around her, and perused the notes she'd made on a memo pad, "I gather this means we have the rest of the evening to do a little gambling?"

"I was thinking of something else, actually."

"Actually . . . so was I."

"I was wondering if Reggie daCoit is in Las Vegas right now."

"Believe it or not, that's *not* what I was thinking about."

Belle drummed her fingers on the writing desk. "If he's here, he'd certainly be worth talking to, don't you think?"

"You were asked to come here to help decipher a crossword puzzle, not get tangled up in a probable murder."

Belle regarded him with wide and innocent eyes. "Rosco! How can you suggest I'd even consider—"

"You're right; what could I be thinking of?" He shook his head, reached around her, and picked up the phone. "Okay. If he's here . . . he's here. At Cactus Cal's." Rosco punched zero into the phone and waited for the operator. "Yes, Mr. Reggie daCoit's room, please." It was answered after only one ring, and Rosco went into a practiced routine: "Mr. daCoit, I'm with *Today's Gambler* magazine. My apologies for calling at what must be a painful time for you, but we'd scheduled an article on your famous late uncle some time ago, and Editorial wants to pursue the piece despite the altered circumstances . . . As someone who obviously knew him well, I was wondering if you might be able to spare a few minutes and share your thoughts? If it isn't too much to ask . . . ?" Rosco looked at Belle, then returned his focus to the phone. Flattery was the best approach in these situations. Everyone liked seeing their name in print. "I'm hoping you can supply some personal details . . . maybe, what it was like to be related to someone so well known in the city? Oh, that's super . . . Could we meet"—Rosco flipped through the Cactus Cal's brochure—"in Gila Gil's Grill, say in a half an hour? Great . . . I'll be with my intern. She's a very pretty young blond woman. We'll see you then."

"Intern?" Belle remarked the moment Rosco hung up the phone.

"That way it won't seem odd if you ask some questions as well . . . I notice you didn't have any problems with the *very pretty* and the *young* part."

GILA Gil's Grill was located on the third floor of the hotel and seemed to be a transplanted tract of land from Death Valley. The walls were faced with rough-hewn red desert rock; and pebble-stoned walkways weaved in and out of small cactus groves and arroyos, allowing each seating area a feeling of seclusion that was almost unmarred by the slot machines set beside the individual tables. Elevated at the room's center, as if on a natural plateau, was a horseshoe-shaped bar also fashioned from desert stone. Ceramic lizard heads poked out from the crevices while behind the bar stood the eatery's namesake: a huge gila monster formed from clay, resin, and a substance that resembled rhinoceros hide. It was ten feet high and thirty feet long, and was surrounded by a number of stuffed gophers in various, life-like poses. Despite every effort at realism, the desert, the real 110-degree desert, could have been a million miles away, but perhaps that was because the three barmaids and waitstaff—also all female—sported the skimpiest of two-piece costumes. Unlike the lobby staff, Gila Gil's were already attired for the Christmas season: red uniforms trimmed with furry white fringe.

After strolling the stone walkways for a minute or two, Belle and Rosco found Reggie daCoit. He was just as he'd described himself: late twenties, slight of build, carrot red hair already thinning. He wore faded jeans, a denim shirt, and a black leather vest with a large Arizona state flag stitched onto the back. An untouched, aqua blue drink with a green paper umbrella sat on the table in front of him. Reggie's attention was devoted solely to his personal slot machine.

"Mr. daCoit?" Rosco said. Reggie slid pale, mistrustful eyes in the intruder's direction, but didn't immediately reply, so Rosco extended his hand. "Bo Dakota, *Today's Gambler.* We sure do appreciate your giving us some time. This is my intern, Ann Jones."

Reggie's thin face broke into a leering grin that revealed tobacco-stained and yellowed teeth. "*The Devil in Miss Jones?*" He extended his hand. "A real film classic. I'm a movie buff, a serious movie buff, if you want to start taking notes, honey . . . Have a seat. And call me Reggie." He patted the chair next to him, but Belle moved to the opposite side of the table, and Rosco sat beside her.

A waitress sidled through the cactus, nearly catching her frothy fringe on the fake thorns. She beamed at the new patrons. "Hi, y'all . . . What'll it be?"

Belle ordered a ginger ale while Rosco asked for a beer. Then he glanced at the slot machine. "How's your luck been running?"

"South," Reggie grumbled.

"Sorry to hear it."

"Ah, it's just nickel stuff . . . Something to pass the time." Reggie snapped his fingers dismissively and chuckled to himself. "Of course, with Dr. Jazz's passing, things are gonna start lookin' up. Yes, indeed."

"My condolences on your loss," was Belle's gentle reply. She seemed sympathy itself.

"Yeah, well . . . one of those things, what can I say? Life, y'know . . . Besides, I stand to pick up about a mil-five after the dust settles. A million-five can mop up a lot of tears. A whole *lotta* tears." Reggie grinned again. It was not a sorrowful expression.

Rosco pulled a notebook from his jacket pocket. "That's the extent of your uncle's legacy?" He made a note. "Interesting . . . Given the fact that the great Dr. Jazz was such an institution in the world of no-limit poker, I would have thought he was worth considerably more than that. It was my understanding that his winnings were three hundred grand alone the night before he died."

"Nah, man . . . Uncle Dave was incorporated—*Vegas style.* You know how that works, dude. He hardly ever played with his own jack. He had backers. They owned his pots—they took the losses, they took the winnings, and Dr.

Jazz took his cut . . . Sure, sometimes he'd roll out his own wad, but he was a careful man. Me? I ain't never been careful, that's my big problem. I'm a reckless kinda' guy, what can I say? I like to take my chances wherever I find 'em." He winked at Belle, then looked back at Rosco. His manner reverted from boastful optimism to one of wounded injustice. "See, Dr. Jazz knew he had some fish in the line last week, and he hooked 'em for himself. Big-time."

Belle was also taking notes. "*Vegas style* . . . That's good. It has a clever ring to it . . . We could use that as a tag line, or maybe even a lead-in, don't you think, *Bo*? If that's acceptable to you, Mr. daCoit?"

"Reggie."

"Reggie." Belle graced him with a sweet and grateful smile.

"Yeah . . . quote whatever ya want, honey. I just made that up . . . that *Vegas-style* thing. You can write that in the mag. Tell your readers all about Reggie daCoit. Don't forget the movie thing."

Belle smiled anew. "Thank you . . . So, you were with your uncle just before he died? And you and he were close enough to share . . . ?"

"Well . . . No. Not exactly. I was in L.A. But I heard who he was playin' with . . . A bunch of chumps . . . They ain't a lotta secrets in Vegas."

"So I hear." Belle said. "Perhaps I should get their names, though? They might be worth chatting with for the article."

"Hey, doll, I don't know no *names*. A couple a' dudes from Seattle. That's all I know."

Belle continued to take notes. "I understand the police

believe your uncle might have been murdered." She looked at Reggie; empathy etched her brow.

"Life in the city, doll. Life in the big, scary city. Happens every day here in Vegas."

The waitress arrived with the drink order. Rosco signed the tab *Bo Dakota* in such a way that it vaguely resembled *B. Graham,* scribbled *Suite 1014,* and said, "Of course, you're aware that your uncle's latest winnings are missing, aren't you?"

Reggie stiffened. "What's all this got to do with *Today's Gambler?*"

Belle assumed another sympathetic pose. "Well, Mr. . . . Reggie . . . I'm sorry to admit this, but murder sells magazines. It's the sad truth about today's media environment. I guess that's why Editorial decided to push the story rather than kill it. I apologize if that seems insensitive—"

"Let me get a little background," Rosco interjected. "Your uncle was born here, in Vegas?"

"Nah, Reno."

"And where does the moniker 'Dr. Jazz' come from?"

"I don't know . . . He played piano in a band when he first got here. I guess that's where he picked it up."

"Any other relatives?"

"Nope. His sister, my mom, died when I was thirteen."

"That's tough," Rosco said.

Reggie's tone fell to a near whisper as he fed another dollar bill into the slot machine. "Yeah, it's tough."

"Who's Gabby?" Belle's question startled both men.

Reggie sat bolt upright; his narrow shoulders jittered. "Where'd you hear about Gabby?"

"I think we got it on the wire service, didn't we, *Bo*?"

"Ah, yeah," Rosco stuttered. "What can you tell us about Gabby?"

"Who are you people?" Reggie shot back. His pale eyes raced from face to face; his gaunt cheeks twitched.

"*Today's Gamb—*"

"You didn't hear about Gabby on no stinkin' wire service of no stinkin' mag—"

"Yes, we—"

Reggie glowered as he purposefully sucked the remainder of his blue drink through the straw. "That *Vegas style* I mentioned a while back? That's for my use only, doll. It's not for publication." He stood with all the fierceness of a small and insignificant man, and stormed out of the restaurant.

"So," Rosco said after he'd disappeared, "care to tell me who Gabby is?"

"There's a straight flush framed on the wall in Dr. Jazz's suite. It's signed *Gabby.*"

"Huh . . . Seems to have struck a nerve."

"And I have a question for you."

"Shoot."

"How come you get to be someone cool like *Bo Dakota,* and I get stuck with *Ann Jones*?"

"Okay, next time you get to pick the names."

BELLE and Rosco spent the better part of the evening strolling through Cactus Cal's and hashing over the snippets of information they'd picked up from Hollister and Reggie daCoit. Hollister's theory that the killer had not found the three hundred thousand dollars seemed logical, leaving the two unknown men from Seattle as the primary suspects, but they'd left town earlier in the week.

By the time Belle and Rosco had finished dinner, it was nearly eleven P.M., two in the morning by East Coast time, and they were exhausted. They dragged themselves back to their suite, took showers, and slid into bed, hoping some answers would come their way the next morning during their visit to the Blue Diamond Animal Shelter.

"You know, we've been here all day and we haven't played one single slot machine?" Belle said as Rosco made an attempt to give her a kiss.

"So?"

"Well, it just seems wrong. Las Vegas is all about gambling, right?"

"But you're not a gambler. Besides, only the casinos win at slots."

Instead of responding, Belle rolled out of bed, walked over to the dresser, and picked up two quarters that were lying next to Rosco's wallet. "I'll be right back. There's a machine at the end of the hall."

"You're kidding me?"

"No. I can't go to bed without at least trying my luck once." She wrapped herself in a hotel robe and trotted out the door while Rosco sat up in bed and shook his head. Belle was back in three minutes, holding the hem of the robe up to her waist. She walked over to Rosco's side of the bed and dropped the hem, releasing an avalanche of quarters onto the floor. Rosco sat up farther in bed.

Belle stepped over the pile of money, crawled on top of

him, and gave him a long kiss. "The trick," she said after their lips parted, "is to quit while you're ahead."

NINE A.M. found Belle and Roscoe southwest of Las Vegas, in Blue Diamond, Nevada, at the animal shelter, where Karen Wise greeted them like long-lost friends. Her manner, her whole being, was so relaxed and affable that Belle couldn't imagine a person or creature not taking comfort in her kindly presence. As for age, Belle couldn't venture a guess; Karen's stature as well as a certain mature and thoughtful presence indicated that she could have been in her sixties or early seventies, but her youthful appearance, her curly, dark hair only slightly flecked with white, and her high energy could have belonged to a woman in her middle to late forties. The woman's enthusiasm and joy were positively contagious; it was obvious to Belle that Karen Wise was incapable of harming a single thing, let alone committing a murder.

She led Rosco and Belle through the shelter, stopping briefly to pat, talk to, coo at, examine, or mildly reprimand her many charges. She also introduced the couple to a volunteer assistant, a man of equally indeterminate age who was as upbeat and as friendly as his "boss." Finally, Karen conducted the couple to Blue Diamond's office for a cup of her special sun tea—a concoction laced with rosemary and mint. The room, like the rest of the building, was teeming with wildlife: healing birds in cages, desert turtles and young jackrabbits also on the mend, and three orphaned coyote pups squabbling over the rights to a tattered dish rag.

"You're aware that Lieutenant Hollister considers you a suspect?" Rosco said in a tone that indicated he thought the idea absurd.

"He's a very mistrustful man." Karen waved a sun-burnt hand as though casually brushing off a fly. "Always has been, poor guy. Uptight. Rigid. It can't be easy being his 'little lady.' "

Belle laughed. It was clear Karen Wise had been the recipient of Hollister's not-so-subtle put-downs. Then she sighed. "I feel terrible that I haven't been able to come up with a solution to this mystery of yours . . . Although I imagine disposing of Dr. Jazz's painting collection should bring you a handsome—"

"I so dislike that term, 'Dr. Jazz,' " Karen protested. "He was a fine person, a true friend to us here . . . but the name made him sound like a thug. Of course, I never much cared for his other choice either."

"Dave Narone wasn't his real name?" Rosco asked.

"Oh no. His real name is daCoit, same as his nephew. He changed it when he moved down here." Karen shooed a fledgling roadrunner away from her tea glass. "Beat it, Otto. You don't drink tea." Otto paid no attention to the injunction, instead pecking noisily on the glass while Karen raised indulgent eyebrows and continued her recitation. "As far as the artwork is concerned, it's nice of you to imagine the stuff is valuable, but the truth is I did those oils myself. They were intended as a 'thank-you' from the shelter. I daresay they're hardly worth the canvas they're painted on—

unless some high-priced gallery suddenly discovers Karen Wise."

"Oh . . ." Belle murmured. "But they're really good."

"Nice of you to say so." Karen shrugged her shoulders. "I like keeping busy, that's all."

At that moment, Otto landed on Belle's lap and settled in as though he'd found the perfect nest.

Karen chortled. "Don't mind him. He's very friendly. They're in the cuckoo family, roadrunners, did you know that? *Geococcyx californianus.*"

Belle looked down at the still-fluffy bird with the bold and inquisitive stare. "So I see." She thought for a long moment. "So the shelter inherits nothing . . ."

"Not unless I get discovered as a latter-day Grandma Moses . . . Or those 'non-liquid' assets miraculously turn up."

The three sat in gloomy silence; only Otto and the other rescued creatures seemed unperturbed by the discouraging news.

"Did Mr. daCoit ever talk about someone named Gabby?"

"Gabby . . . Gabby . . . Oh, yes . . . I believe there was a lady friend some time ago . . . I think he told me they broke up on account of his arthritis. Very sad—and selfish, on her part. Bodies can be ailing. It doesn't mean the spirit is." Karen sighed. "He made such a fuss over those 'non-liquid' assets . . ." She lifted her head. "Well, no use crying over spilled milk . . . though to tell you the truth, things are going to be real tough around here without his annual gifts.

Our volunteers are wonderful, but food and medication don't come cheap."

Belle also released a sigh. "I still believe you're right about the crossword puzzle, Karen. Mr. daCoit clearly had a reason for making the instructions so cryptic. Perhaps, as he suggested, it was to keep his nephew from finding the money first."

Rosco nodded. "If those 'assets' were *not* located in the suite at Cactus Cal's, they'd belong to Reggie . . . Do you have any idea how much money we're talking about, Karen?"

" 'A lot' was all I was told. I never thought to ask for details."

"So, we have to assume the legacy intended for the shelter is still in his suite . . . maybe in the form of securities." Belle looked at Rosco for confirmation, but his response wasn't encouraging:

"I doubt we'll find any such documents. If someone *did* make off with the three hundred thousand dollars in winnings, he or she would have pocketed any other paperwork that appeared valuable."

"Well, that's it then," Karen said after another long and painful pause. She looked at Otto and then at the various cages with their various hopping or fluttering inhabitants, and then finally mustered a smile as she turned to Belle. "Thanks for trying to help."

Rosco stood. "We're going to head back to Las Vegas. If the money's still in that suite, we'll find it, Karen, don't worry."

Belle placed Otto in Karen Wise's capable hands.

"You can keep him if you want, Belle . . . He needs a good home."

"We have a dog . . . Besides, I don't know what roads he'd run on in our neighborhood."

Karen glanced down at the three coyote pups who were still wrangling over the dish rag. "Otto can handle himself. In the city or the country."

ON the drive back to Cactus Cal's, Belle and Rosco discussed gaining access to Dr. Jazz's hotel suite, deciding that the best approach was for Rosco to jimmy the lock, while Belle stood lookout downstairs in case Lieutenant Hollister opted to return. But as they crossed the hotel lobby, their plan was dealt a blow. Exiting the elevator were two uniformed LVMPD policemen. Between them was Reggie daCoit. He was in handcuffs.

"What's going on, Officer?" Rosco asked as they passed.

"What's it look like? We're making an arrest," one of the cops groused as they marched the prisoner away. DaCoit kept his head bowed; his greasy red hair and scrawny neck seemed to radiate both guilt and hopelessness.

Belle and Rosco stepped onto the elevator and pushed TEN. When the door opened on the tenth floor, they were greeted by another uniformed officer. "Sorry, folks, this is a crime scene. Please step back onto the elevator."

"But our room is on this floor," Belle protested.

"Sorry, ma'am."

"Let 'em pass, Hank." The order came from Hollister,

who was standing at the entrance to Suite 1015. Rosco and Belle walked down to meet him.

"What's up, Lieutenant?"

Hollister tilted his head toward the doorway, and the three of them stepped into Dr. Jazz's suite. His baby grand piano had been smashed to pieces. A crowbar lay on the carpet beside it.

"I gather Reggie daCoit did this?" Rosco asked.

"The people in the suite next door called to complain about the noise, so the house detective came up. He found our boy beating the life out of the piano while mumbling, 'Come to Daddy, Gabby . . .' The guy had really lost it. By the time I got here, Reggie confessed to the whole sheebang—strychnine, the works."

"So, Gabby is . . . a *piano*?" Belle wondered aloud.

Hollister only shrugged.

"A piano who 'left because of his arthritis.' " Belle glanced at the far side of the room. The framed straight flush had been pulled from the wall and smashed across the writing desk. The backing had been ripped off and the five cards were scattered on the carpet.

"Looks like Reggie was searching for something," Rosco said. "Did he find it?"

Hollister shook his head. "No . . . But interestingly enough, I ran an IRS check on the good 'doctor.' Paid his taxes just like Johnny B. Good. His net worth was estimated at six million."

Rosco let out a low whistle. "So if his bank accounts are only showing one-point-five mil, you're saying there's another four and a half million dollars stashed in this suite somewhere?"

"And it sure as heck ain't in the piano, is it?" Hollister tossed in.

"But how could he hide it?" Rosco asked. "That kind of cash has to take up a fair amount of space."

Belle walked over to the smashed picture frame, bent down, and picked up one of the cards. "Why is the piano named Gabby?"

The two men looked at one another, but said nothing as Belle continued, almost to herself:

"It's an anagram . . . Gabby—Baby G. Baby grand . . ."

"And?" Hollister said.

"Can I see that piece of paper Narone left, Lieutenant?"

Hollister pulled the note from his pocket and handed it to Belle, who studied it for several long and silent minutes. "It's all anagrams . . . even his name, Dave Narone—Reno Nevada . . . And *Still, Man Wasted Talent*—Last will and testament . . . And his instructions—they indicate that: 'A puzzle grid must be created by one Anna Graham.' I don't know how we missed that clue . . . If he knew my work— and he obviously did—he must have realized I'm called Belle, not Anna. Second: 'there is good reason to—fear of it, however cute.' 'Fear of it, however cute . . .' I thought it was an odd warning, but the sentence is also an anagram, and it tells us exactly the form these mysterious 'liquid assets' take. 'Fear of it, however cute'—Ace, two, three, four, five. 'Gabby's' straight flush. That's it! It's in the cards!" Belle was so excited by her discovery that the inadvertent pun didn't even make her wince.

Rosco glanced at the card in his hand and said, "Diamonds . . . Of course . . . You could stick four million dollars' worth of diamonds in a catsup bottle if you wanted. They'd have to be flawless, and the right cut, to be worth that much, but you could do it."

Hollister began walking around the room. "Kinda' like finding a needle in a haystack. Four mil in stones could be anywhere—sewn into his clothes, under the carpet, in the couch cushions . . ."

"I don't think so," was Belle's immediate response. "This list of words I was given; SHOE is an anagram for HOSE, and FLOG is an anagram for GOLF, RETAILS is an anagram for REALIST, and so forth, meaning I created a puzzle using *anagrams* rather than the correct solutions." As Hollister continued to look perplexed, Belle added, "I used the wrong words, Lieutenant . . . but I'm betting the correct ones will reveal the dead man's final wishes in a message we can actually decipher."

"Except you're not a gambling person," Rosco observed.

"*Wasn't* a gambling person." Belle smiled and raised her eyebrows while Hollister asked a still unconvinced:

"How long will it take to make a new crossword?"

"An hour or two. The length of the words will remain consistent, so I'll be able to use my same puzzle grid."

Hollister picked up the phone, punched in a few numbers, and ordered coffee from room service. "Anything to eat with it?" he asked Belle and Rosco.

Belle chuckled. "How about whatever comes 'on a roll'?"

ACROSS

1. Clear tables
4. TV network
7. Ruth & Rose wood?
10. Santa helper
13. St. John's island
15. Not the up-and-up
16. New; comb. form
17. Message, part 1
19. Cookie pot
20. Links sport
21. Eke out
22. Show girl's need
23. Blow up; abbr.
24. Bristle
25. Cable; e.g.
26. Message, part 3
29. Old gas sign
31. Cut glass
32. Casino watering hole
33. Phoenix to Flagstaff dir.
34. Casino dance room
36. Pampering; abbr.
37. Japanese crater or park
38. Give the boot
39. Mr. Bishop
40. Message, part 4
44. Mr. Big-bucks
45. N.C. School
46. Moon vehicle
49. Tromped
50. Famous fountain
52. Phone or bucks lead-in
53. Crew member; abbr.
54. Message, part 6
56. Scrap
57. And so on; abbr.
58. Paint by numbers guy?
59. Ship's letters
60. Owed
61. Draft org.
62. Pig quarters

DOWN

1. Sheriff's shield
2. On the Blue side?
3. Put off
4. Past
5. Jumper's prop
6. West Pointers
7. Fink out
8. Breezy
9. 20-Across gadget
10. Fun
11. Rated G
12. Message, part 2
14. World financial org.
18. Many a main drag
22. Holds
24. 25-Across listing
25. Hebrew letter
26. Literary monogram
27. Stock sale: abbr.
28. Sgt. or cpl.
29. Trappers
30. Winter footwear
34. Idiot's reply
35. Practitioner; suffix
36. Rocky peak
37. Message, part 5
38. Betting parlor; abbr.
39. Mr. Bon Jovi
41. Sailing class; abbr.

🌴 Still, Man Wasted Talent 🌴

42. Young cels
43. Orates
46. Some jeans
47. Discharge
48. Mr. Robbins

50. Ballet skirt
51. Wedding chapel prop
52. One of the Blancs
54. Up and coming; abbr.
55. _____ Vegas

The Eraser's Edge

*G*ARROTE, burke, throttle, asphyxiate . . . How many letters might you need for a synonym for 'strangle' . . . ? Or you could make the puzzle clue 'strangler' and widen the field to include other types of murder . . . a Thug or Thugee—the ancient Hindu sect of assassins . . . a 'Jack Ketch,' which is, of course, British slang for an executioner—who could also be a hangman, topsman, or topping cove . . . Or perhaps you might consider adjusting the grid slightly . . ." The remarks came from a large man sitting beside a roaring fire on the second-floor parlor of the handsome old El Tovar Hotel, the famed stone and wood-beamed "lodge" perched on the edge of the Grand Canyon's south rim. The fact that the man was confined to a wheelchair seemed to have no effect on his broad and magisterial presence; quite the opposite. To Joe Conrad, his mobile chair was a roving throne—a *howdah,* as he liked to jest with his deep and lordly laugh. "An Americanized *howdah* for an ex-cattle rancher who hooked up with a bum steer . . . And how's that for a fine how-do-you-do . . ."

The reply to Conrad's minimonologue came from Jean O'Neal. She was seated at a nearby desk, and bent over a sheet of graph paper, penciling in the initial design for a new crossword puzzle. "I'm not sure, Joe . . . Maybe I should change the solution to plain old KILL—"

"With the clue being either 'slay,' 'erase,' 'veto,' 'defeat,' 'suppress,' 'huggermugger'—"

" 'Huggermugger'?" Jean's hazel eyes crinkled in a smile as she turned to reply. Like Joe, she was comfortably ensconced in later middle age; her gray hair was tinted an exuberant lilac hue that matched the vibrant blues and mauves and purples she favored in her dress. Also like Joe, she dearly loved to laugh—which she did with happy abandon.

"Origin unknown. Noun, adjective, verb: transitive and intransitive denoting secrecy, confusion, something jumbled or disorderly . . . an act conferred in a stealthy manner."

"KILL is a touch oversimplistic, don't you think, Jean?" It was Will Mawme who had joined the conversation. Where Joe was solid and hearty—despite his inability to work his legs properly—Will was bony and slight of build, so fragile-looking it seemed as if only his abundant nervous energy kept him in motion, or even alive and breathing. A half-smoked cheroot dangled eternally from his lips, never appearing to grow shorter or longer, as if in a perpetual state of suspended animation. Mawme was also a puzzler without par, and the prime organizer of the group's annual crossword

competition, celebration, and charity fund-raiser for the
Phoenix Literacy Programme. It was Will Mawme who had
originally decreed the yearly gala be held on New Year's
Eve; it was he who traditionally constructed a "surprise first-
night lexical conundrum"; it was he who dictated how the
New Year's Day competition should be judged, and who
the event's guest of honor would be.

Mawme now turned his thin, intense face to that guest
of honor—none other than famed crossword editor Belle
Graham, who was curled up on a sofa thumbing through
one of her favorite books—a volume of the *Encyclopaedia
Britannica*: this one copyright 1929. The El Tovar Hotel
had a library almost as venerable as its many gabled building. "Don't you agree that KILL is overly simplistic as a
solution. Or, I daresay, even as a clue." Mawme shifted his
cigar from one corner of his mouth to the other as he spoke.

Arriving with her husband, Rosco, just prior to a lunch-
eon in the hotel's well-appointed dining room, Belle had
had several hours to observe the gathering's eight attendees.
It hadn't taken long to intuit their relationships. Mawme,
she'd discerned, held sway simply because no one would
openly challenge his autocratic and often cutting manner—
skills he'd honed in Arizona's courtrooms while serving as
one of the state's most cutthroat prosecutors. But finding
fault with Jean O'Neal's word choice, Belle realized, was
bound to bring a swift counterattack from Joe. It was clear
he considered Jean more than a friend.

As Belle had surmised, Joe immediately came to Jean's
defense. "What would you employ, Mawme? EXECU-
TION?"

Will turned a tight, tense face toward the bigger man. "Execution—*if* it were to fit into the crossword Jean is constructing—would enable her clue to be more ambiguous, and thus more entertaining . . . anything from 'capital punishment' to 'completion' to a musical reference . . . But then we, and our words, are always slaves to the grid we have created."

"Precisely why I like KILL better," Joe all but growled. "Killjoy . . . Killing time, killdeer; the options seem endless—and let us not forget Jean-Claude Killy!"

"Kill the fatted calf," put in Belle. She'd meant to ease the friction, but then winced remembering how the disabled man had met his fate—a tumble from a quarter-horse while roping a young steer.

"Or the goose that lays the golden egg," Jean added quickly. She smiled beatifically upon the group, but it was Joe who received the full force of this tender expression.

"The twins," Ginger and Tommy Wolfe, looked up from a jigsaw puzzle they were assembling on a tabletop at the room's center. "Fables," they said almost in unison. Ginger and her brother were travel agents. They owned their own business, and it was they who arranged the crossworders' yearly excursions. True to her name, Ginger was a redhead, as was Tommy although his once wavy locks were now thinning and his hairline receding. Brother and sister had the pink complexion of ripe peaches, but their bodies were shaped like two matching pears. They had not spent more than a few days apart in their forty-eight years on earth.

" 'Fabulous' quotations . . ." Ginger Wolfe enthused, putting aside the unfinished depiction of the Grand Canyon at sunset. "Let's test our communal knowledge. After all, a crossword is only as good as the quotes and quips within the solutions. In this case, let's rely on old Aesop—"

Tommy took up his sibling's challenge. "Okay, here goes . . . from *The Hare and the Tortoise*: 'Slow and steady wins the race.' "

"*The Lion and the Mouse*," put in Jean. " 'No act of kindness, no matter how small, is ever wasted.' "

" 'Familiarity breeds contempt': *The Fox and the Lion*," interjected Mawme with his patronizing smile; while Joe Conrad, still smarting over Jean's perceived snub, countered with an austere and basso:

" 'Any excuse will serve a tyrant': *The Wolf and the Lamb*."

"If you're on the subject of wolves," shot back Will, "don't forget *The Wolf in Sheep's Clothing*—"

"The one about appearances being deceiving?" interrupted Ginger. "Our mother loved to quote that when we were little, and were still able to fool the neighbors as to which of us was which . . . the 'Twin Wolves' we were called."

The remainder of the group: Hunter Evans, D.C. Irving, and Gwen Beckstein entered the room at that moment, stamping the remaining tufts of snow from their hiking boots. Their afternoon walk had taken them to the Bright Angel Trailhead, but with a winter's early sunset impending, they'd turned back without beginning to descend the switchback trail that led toward the distant Colorado River.

"Are we on lists of animals?" D.C. asked as he rubbed his hands by the fire. He had a deft smile and a wide-open manner acquired from a life spent out of doors. He was an

Arizonan born and bred, a man whose eyes reflected the solitude of cactus and scrub, and roads traversing mile upon mile of uninhabited land. Despite his cowboy appearance and laconic manner, D.C. was a successful golf pro, an institution at a high-end Scottsdale resort.

"No, the twins suggested 'fabulous quotations' . . . so we started on an Aesop binge," Jean answered with a laugh, before turning to Hunter. "It's too bad Mary Ann came down with the flu, and had to miss the festivities this year. I always enjoy spending time with her. I love that British accent . . . I guess in part because it refuses to go away. Even after all these years."

Hunter shook his head. "My wife's the one who's usually healthy as an ox, but she really got hit hard this time . . . I insisted on staying home with her, but she wouldn't hear of it. She also claimed she was glad to be 'spared our verbal badinage' for once."

Jean laughed her bright and pleasant laugh once more. "I can just hear her saying that." Then her expression turned pensive. "I don't like to think of loved ones being separated at the beginning of another year. John's not with us, either." She looked at Gwen. John was Gwen's husband.

"A workaholic . . . what can I say? There's a team of Japanese businessmen flying into Tucson tomorrow. It could result in some major input for our Sandstone Estates project."

"Still . . ." Jean persisted, but Gwen shrugged off the effort at sympathy:

"Someone has to pay the bills."

There was something aggressive in Gwen's tone, something raw that jangled the nerves. Everyone felt it; for a moment no one—including Mawme—spoke.

It was Belle who broke the awkward silence. "The crossword you're working on now, Jean, will it be part of tomorrow's competition?"

"No. It's just something she started playing around with," Mawme stated in Jean's stead.

"She's doing more than 'playing around,' " Joe snorted.

Mawme raised his eyebrows. "I presume we're all 'playing around' when it comes to word *games,* Joe. I certainly don't consider this work."

Again, tension descended upon the room, and again, it was Belle who dispelled it. "Well, I consider it work," she said in a cheery tone. "Not unpleasant work; I certainly enjoy myself, but constructing and editing crossword puzzles *is* my bread and butter." She smiled at Gwen, D.C., and Hunter Evans, then at the twins—while carefully avoiding the nettlesome trio of Mawme, Conrad, and Jean O'Neal. "Now, if you'll excuse me, I'm going to see if I can find that husband of mine. Shake him away from the TV and his football game so we can admire the famous sunset hitting those gorgeous red 'Temple' rock formations . . . We'll see you all at dinner."

"Libations at seven-thirty," Mawme interjected. "Dinner promptly at eight-fifteen—with my special yearly offering dessert."

"Yes, indeed." Belle smiled again, although she was beginning to wish she hadn't accepted the group's invitation. As tempting as three days at the Grand Canyon had seemed, misgivings about the gathering were starting to stir in her brain. Something unpleasant was afoot, and it seemed to be pointing to a fight between one frail but power-obsessed man and another confined to a wheelchair.

DINNER was indeed festive, the dining room's massive stone fireplaces ablaze, flowers and greenery bedecking each table, a rolling simmer of conversation spicing the air along with the dense perfumes of rich winter foods: mulled wines, savory soups, roasts heaped with potatoes, and glazed root vegetables. The conversation at the puzzlers' special table was no less heady. Homonyms, synonyms, antonyms, and anagrams flew about with the alacrity of lexical light. Everyone seemed determined to trump a dinner partner. *Double entendres* and puns rocketed across the white linen and laden plates. The only person immune to the verbal one-upsmanship was Rosco, who sat beside Belle with an amused expression tugging at the corners of his mouth.

"A penny for your thoughts," she whispered.

"Too cheap, by far."

"I gather you're not daydreaming about words."

"Depends which ones you've got in mind."

Then Belle's attention was commandeered by Will Mawme, who announced that his much-anticipated crossword would be distributed after coffee and dessert. But he added a new caveat to the procedure: This year the puzzle was in a sealed envelope and to be completed not in each other's company, but in the privacy of the attendees' bedrooms—after the stroke of midnight.

Belle gave Rosco's foot a conspiratorial nudge. They'd

have the first few moments of the new year to themselves, after all.

WITH "Auld Lang Syne" sung, and "Good night's" and "Happy New Year's" exchanged, Rosco and Belle crossed the porch leading toward the hotel's lawn and the canyon's south rim. The couple was silent in the vastness of the night, the daubs of snow dotting the craggy rocks that stood sentinel over the great black chasm that had been scoured and rent by eons of river water attacking its rocky walls. Here and there in the building's long shadow, deer stood nuzzling the ice and snow in search of hidden grass, but they were also quiet; and if they glanced at Belle and Rosco at all, it was with an untroubled stare. Not one of them took flight. Instead they moved soundlessly among the junipers and piñon pines that stood ink-dark against the sky.

"Beautiful," Belle murmured as she huddled close to Rosco. They wrapped their arms around each other and stared into a frosty night that dropped away into the lethal and jagged depths below.

"All those miners working the canyon cliffs," she whispered. "How did they do it? Living halfway up and halfway down . . . What did they eat?"

"Probably not 'double whammy butterscotch pie.' "

"I'm serious, Rosco."

"So am I . . . sort of. The miners, the prospectors like that Louis Boucher fellow who lived out a solo hermit existence . . . explorers who charted the Colorado . . . I was also reading about John Wesley Powell, a guy who lost an arm during the Civil War, continued to fight for the Union, then decided to navigate the Colorado in 1869—only to have nearly half his crew of nine desert him. I'll bet his three months down there fighting the rapids didn't allow for much variety in the cuisine line."

Belle hunched her shoulders in thought. "I'm glad I'm not an explorer—or a prospector or trapper."

"I'm glad you're not, too—not with your sense of direction. I'd never see you again."

Belle chuckled. "At least, I know what to do when confronted with a map. You don't even know how to unfold one."

"Hey, they make great beer coasters if you don't unfold them . . . Look, people who go out to tame the wilderness don't even have maps. That's what make them *explorers*. They navigate by the sun and moon and stars."

She slipped her arm down to squeeze his waist. "And they never order up second helpings of cappuccino mousse."

"It takes a he-man to kill off a couple of moose."

"Don't start, Rosco. I've had enough word play for one night."

"How about a smooch, then? Something else those miners didn't get a whole lot of."

She turned her face to his, but in the midst of their embrace a cloud of mist began advancing from the canyon's edge. At first it was wispy, like steam blowing off a pot of creamed soup; then the mist became fog, which grew in density: a white miasma billowing upward to obscure both the ravine and the path wavering along its treacherous border.

"Time to find higher ground," Rosco said.

"But not necessarily loftier intentions."

WHILE Rosco and Belle retreated to the cozy comfort of their room, another guest in another wing of the hotel was engaged in an anxious and whispered conversation. The mode was via cell phone as the speaker had opted to avoid the El Tovar switchboard. The room was dark, another precaution intended to prevent late revelers in the corridor outside or on the porch below from realizing the inhabitant was still awake.

"But I'm telling you he knows! . . . Yes, I'm sure! . . . He spelled it out in that damn crossword puzzle he landed on us tonight!" The voice cracked with fear and anger.

"What do you mean you've 'got it under control'?" A sharp sigh, a nervous and shallow breath. The tone lowered, but the level of emergency did not.

"No, I'm sure the others don't have a clue . . . They wouldn't. Especially if they didn't know what they're looking for. Unless you—Wait! I hear someone outside the door!" The speaker stood stock still until the laughter weaved off down the hall. Another sigh, this one more panicky than before.

"What should I do? What should *we* do? You tell me . . . I don't want to risk being caught going to his room, but . . . What do you mean, you'll 'take care of it'? . . . That's not possible! You aren't—"

But the connection had been severed.

ACROSS

1. Boston campus; abbr.
4. Pig-poke connector
7. Black bird
10. Likely
13. Fracas
14. Ariz, neighbor
15. Mr. Kingsley
16. Classic car
17. Ladies who go way back; abbr.
18. Hitch hair-raiser
21. Hockey org.
23. Mr. Fassbinder
24. ____Riban
26. Georgia, once; abbr.
27. Windbag?; var.
31. College board member?
33. Airport info
34. Mr. Hunter
35. "Out of____"
36. Wind dir.
37. "I'm all____"
38. Nashville campus; abbr.
39. Lou's partner
40. Arena in 51-Down
41. Den____
43. Randolph Scott film
44. Kindest
47. New Zealand fish
48. Egyptian king
49. Shines again
50. Actress Dyan
52. Meadowlands' athlete
53. Let go
54. Hi-ho's in the Alps
56. Me in Metz
57. Hitch hair-raiser, with "To"
61. It lit Ingrid's light
64. VCR reading
65. Poetically above
66. FBI & ATF cousin
67. Presidential monogram
68. Day-____
69. "The Sacred Wood" poet's monogram
70. Chicago trains
71. Call upon

DOWN

1. Steamed
2. Ms. Lupino
3. Hitch hair-raiser
4. Like JFK Airport
5. Gov. arts support
6. Loath
7. Hillside shelter
8. Newborn
9. "A friend____is . . ."
10. Weapon
11. ____brained.
12. 2000 lbs.
19. "The____of the Worlds"
20. Annoyed Asta utterance
22. Watering
24. Sch. grp.
25. Sandy sound?
26. "Lifeboat" locale
28. Hitch hair-raiser
29. Rhine feeder
30. TV ltrs.
32. Fort Worth campus; abbr.
33. The last word
36. Cloud in Cluny
37. 100 Centavos
39. Preservative; abbr.
40. Smith & Jones film; abbr.
41. Cartoon sot's word
42. "Gotcha!"
43. Counter treats
44. Meadowlands athlete
45. California airport letters
46. Recipe meas.

🌴 There's a Hitch! 🌴

(crossword grid)

48. Like Hades
49. Live
51. Ditty from "Annie"
52. "Weary Blues" poet's monogram
55. To be in Brest
56. Arts degs.

57. Gear tooth
58. Internet co.
59. "The Man Who Knew___ Much"
60. Slippery one
62. Film speed letters
63. Engine additive

ORNING found the hotel still swathed in fog so thick and cumbrous that all views of the canyon's distant north rim had vanished; and even the south rim trail immediately fronting El Tovar was completely obscured. Only the few piñons beside the entry portico were visible, but they looked like ghosts, looming eerily out of clouds of suffocating vapor while the ravens perched in the trees' branches squawked and fluttered their wings as if to rid themselves of the air's unaccustomed weight.

Rosco, Belle, and several of the puzzlers who had gathered for breakfast regarded the scene with heavy hearts.

"I guess there won't be any hiking out to Maricopa or Powell Point today," D.C. observed.

"Not unless you want to wind up dead," Hunter Evans answered. "I'd stepped outside when this fog blew in last night . . . You know, there's not much in the way of a guard rail in some spots on the trail."

"We were outside, too," Belle began, "near the—"

"Guess we must have missed spotting each other in that pea soup." Hunter poured himself another cup of coffee. "Where's Will this morning? I'd like to strangle the old buzzard. His crossword kept me up half the night."

"It was a doozie," Jean agreed. "One of his best. Maybe *the* best . . . And for such a Hitchcockian evening; it couldn't have been more perfect. I kept thinking of *North by Northwest* and Cary Grant on Mount Rushmore hanging from some presidential proboscis, with nothing but thin air between him and the rocks below."

The twins appeared with Joe Conrad and Gwen Beckstein. Only Joe seemed unperturbed at the inclement weather. "Saves me from making a fool of myself doing wheelies around that pueblo watchtower out at Desert View." He smiled at Jean. "Sleep well?"

"Like a log."

Joe glanced up at one of the massive, hand-hewn logs crisscrossing the ceiling, "Sure hope those beams don't fall 'asleep' on the job."

"Well, who's for a little friendly puzzle competition?" Tommy Wolfe asked the group in general.

"Will's not here yet—" his sister began, but her words were curtailed by a sudden commotion in the lobby below. Park rangers and a rescue squad crowded into the reception area, and then hurried out while the guests watched in growing apprehension.

"Someone fell over the edge . . ." The murmur passed

from person to person as it reached the second-floor sitting room and flowed down the halls of the old hotel and into every room.

"No body to be seen . . . just dislodged rocks . . ."

"Then how do they know . . . ?"

"Boot marks in the snow . . . broken tree branches . . . traces of blood . . ."

Two park rangers returned in an attempt to allay the guests' fears, but their news caused only greater consternation. A person was "presumed" to have lost his or her footing on the canyon trail. Evidence indicated a last-minute "effort at survival," but "attempts to verbally raise the victim had proven futile," and "the fog was inhibiting rescue efforts."

And then came the most worrisome disclosure: Did anyone know of a guest who was missing?

Tommy Wolfe looked at his sister. "I'll call Will's room," she said. "I'm sure he simply overslept."

GWEN Beckstein was weeping so copiously, the hotel's other residents cast sheepish, uneasy glances at the huddled group of puzzlers. Gwen didn't mind what they or anyone else thought of her behavior. "He must be dead," she kept repeating between her sobs. "It's so cold out there, and he's so . . . so delicate. He couldn't survive even if—"

"Don't torture yourself, Gwen." It was Joe whose soothing voice sought to comfort her.

"What do you care! You never liked him anyway!"

Joe Conrad regarded her, his face somber and sad. "You're not being reasonable, Gwen."

Her tone, husky with tears, turned snappish. "Why should I be? Why should anyone be 'reasonable' when an old friend dies? I was the one who always aided Will with this yearly shindig. Chose a charity to benefit from our largesse. Helped picked a fun and interesting locale so the twins could—" Sobs overwhelmed her again.

Ginger Wolfe took Gwen's hand. "We don't know Will's dead."

Gwen's eyes hardened in irritation. "You've seen the signs posted all over this hideous place . . . DANGER . . . BEWARE OF FALLING ROCKS. And DANGEROUS OVERLOOK—DO NOT ENTER right where he went off? Why would he go near there? The park rangers told us that hikers regularly—" The words broke off. "Oh, I wish we'd never come! Will was so excited about spending New Year's at the Grand Canyon . . . I wish I'd never listened to him, though. I wish none of us had!"

Ginger looked at her brother, who then turned to Hunter Evans, taking him aside to murmur a *sotto voce:* "Should we try to contact John, do you think? Gwen's taking this awfully hard. Business deal or no, maybe he should be here with her?"

"With this weather, the only way he could get here would be to drive; even in the best of conditions, Tucson is . . ." The statement went unfinished.

With Will Mawme's friends understandably preoccupied, Belle and Rosco remained at the periphery, neither part of the prevailing fear and sorrow, but also not wholly removed from the situation. "I'm wondering if we should just pack up and head home?" Rosco said when they'd sufficiently distanced themselves from the group. "I get the sense we're intruding on some very personal space."

Belle shook her head. "I would feel as if I were deserting everyone."

"But what can you do, Belle?"

"Hang tight, I guess. Wait and see?"

LUNCH came and went; the afternoon wore on, and the fog became an increasingly menacing presence. Every window was shrouded in evil grayish white; no one ventured out of doors, not even onto the normally welcoming porches. The puzzlers drifted together and apart, few spoke; the reality of death was becoming unavoidable.

In the midst of this gloom, Belle sat in a chair in the first-floor reception area. A fire was crackling in the large stone hearth; the hotel guests unacquainted with Will Mawme and his party were wandering in and out of the lobby gift shop, chatting, laughing, and enjoying themselves. Rosco was in the TV lounge with six other guests, glued to the tube, watching some beefy men in football pads throw themselves at a group of equally sizable specimens, and Belle was—working a crossword in front of one of the roaring fireplaces. It was the puzzle Mawme had constructed for the previous evening—the one everyone had been instructed to save until after midnight.

Her favorite red pen had just marked the final solution when the nib caught the paper and sent it spinning to the floor, where it landed face up and turned outward into the rest of the room. Belle bent to retrieve it, and suddenly noticed letters that seemed to contain a very recognizable word. The letters were on the diagonal running from lower left to upper right, not far from the puzzle's center.

Belle put the crossword in her lap, and looked across the room. Her eyes were bright and fixed. "HUNTER," she murmured and stood. It never occurred to her to find Rosco and explain this strange discovery. Instead, she went in search of Mr. Evans himself.

"BUT your name is right here." Belle pushed the crossword in Evans's direction. He stood in the doorway to his room, the oak frame dark against the corridor's floral paper, the transom above his head open. Steam and something that smelled like herbal bath salts scented the air. Belle pointed again. "And the message seems to indicate that you—"

"What? That I dragged Will Mawme out of bed, then spirited him through the hotel, took him a quarter of a mile down the trail, and tossed him into the ravine? All without raising a speck of suspicion from the other guests?"

"That's not what I'm suggesting, no."

"Then what are you insinuating, Ms. Graham?" Evans's tone had turned more than frosty.

Belle should have been prepared for the query. She should have been better prepared for the interview on every front, but she'd never been a person fond of precautions or prior planning. "I'm simply stating what's obvious on this piece of paper: GOT YOU HUNTER—"

"And? I would have to have been a fool not to have noticed my own name on the diagonal, Miss Graham. But it means nothing; and I would suggest that it's only some sort of bizarre coincidence."

"I have a hunch that Will Mawme was far too sophisticated a crossword constructor to have had your name appear in his puzzle by accident."

"You want to play detective, do it somewhere else." Evans moved to close the door, then reconsidered. "Will may have been a guy people loved to hate—or hated to love—but he was my friend." The door shut with a firm bang, and Belle turned to find Jean O'Neal standing surprisingly near. Her room key was in her hand.

"Poor Hunter," she said, "This is hitting everyone hard. We're simply responding in different ways." Then Jean noticed the crossword Belle was holding. "One of Will's finest." She teared up and released a mournful sigh. "Hard to believe . . ."

Belle glanced down at the puzzle and made a snap decision: Jean seemed a person she could trust. "Did you happen to notice this message running on the diagonal?" Belle pointed.

Jean removed her bifocals and replaced them with special reading glasses. "Why, no . . . I wonder what that could—?" The words died in her throat. She looked at Hunter Evans's door, then returned a troubled expression to Belle. "But . . . but that would suggest . . . Are you suggesting it was foul play? We're friends, after all . . ."

"Hunter told me that Mawme was a man everyone loved to hate or hated to love."

"That's just talk . . . male bluster, if you will. Oh, yes, Will could be lordly; he could be dictatorial and supremely difficult at times, but no one hated him." Jean tried to smile. "Not even Joe! Although those two large egos certainly enjoyed going head to head." She sighed deeply again, and handed the crossword back to Belle. "I'm aware that you enjoy a bit of a reputation as a sleuth . . . and that your husband is a private investigator . . . but for the sake of some very jangled nerves, perhaps it's best if you keep any suspicions to yourself." Her eyes shone with kindly concern, but Belle began to notice something tougher and more steely beneath the surface. "Poor, dear Gwen Beckstein's beside herself. The twins feel at fault for arranging our journey . . . even D.C. is an altered man." Jean took Belle's hand. "Will met with a tragic accident. It's as simple as that. The park rangers and the rescue team say it's an all too common occurrence."

IN typical fashion, Belle was beginning to doubt the "tragic accident" theory. Mawme had constructed a puzzle and insisted it be solved in private, meaning the guest for whom the message was intended—*if* it was indeed some form of message—had ample time to reflect on the fact that Mawme was playing a game with them. And *if* there was a secret, and *if* the situation was in any way criminal or unlawful—all very big *if*s, but nonetheless ample reason to suspect that foul play would be a logical follow-up.

She looked at the crossword again, wondered why no one else had recognized the importance of the diagonal line, then immediately recanted her own query. Who was to say each puzzler *hadn't* noticed it? Hunter Evans had, but Jean

O'Neal had seemed surprised. On the other hand, that could have been merely an act. Besides, if Will Mawme had been murdered, someone—and it surely looked like Hunter Evans—knew precisely what Mawme meant by placing the name on the diagonal. Belle decided it was time for a consultation with her husband.

She found him in the TV lounge, where now ten or so viewers were hunched forward in their chairs, silently staring at the screen as a football spiraled in the air above the muddy field, and what looked like an army of bodies flung themselves atop one another. In the muck and mire, it was impossible to tell one team's uniforms from another's. Within the human wreckage, no one seemed remotely concerned with the whereabouts of the ball.

"Want to take a walk, Rosco?" Belle whispered.

No answer.

"Rosco?"

"Sure," he mumbled back.

"Great. Let's peek inside the building Mary Colter designed . . . the one that resembles an ancient pueblo and has the shop selling the native crafts and rugs. We don't have to walk far, or near the canyon's edge—"

"What?"

Belle sighed. Maybe it was a Boston team playing, she reflected, which would account for Rosco's inability to concentrate on anything else under the sun. But then, she wondered if Boston even had a professional football team, and if it did, what its name was. Not the Boston Baked Beans, she decided. The Boston Beans and their half-baked fans . . . She smiled privately at her little joke, then told herself she might need to keep this jest to herself. Besides, it could very well be a college game—making the team The Eggheads with their parboiled cheering section. Belle smiled again. "It's just a few steps, really. We don't have to get close to the rim."

"The rim?" During this exchange, Rosco had never looked at his wife. His focus had remained entirely on the television.

"In the fog . . . during our walk—"

"Walk?"

Belle didn't respond. If the timing wasn't right for a stroll of El Tovar's grounds, it probably wasn't the best moment to discuss a potential homicide, either. "I guess I'll go by myself . . . When does the game end?"

"Shhhh," one of the other fans said with a good deal of annoyance in his voice, "we're trying to watch some football, lady, in case you hadn't noticed."

Rosco was immediately attentive. He glowered at the man. "What did you say to my wife?"

The man turned, noticed the look on Rosco's face, and realized he'd crossed the line. "Ah . . . Sorry, pal. It's just that I'm a big UCLA fan."

Rosco leveled a grim smile at him. "Then chances are you've got a long afternoon ahead of you . . . pal." He stood and strode out of the room with Belle.

HOPI House stood on El Tovar's grounds. Designed by the architect Mary Colter in 1905, it was fashioned from rough reddish stone and other materials native to northern Arizona, and it had a forceful, solid appearance as though it had been part of the landscape for many long centuries—well before the advent of explorers, prospectors, miners, and crossword aficionados.

Belle and Rosco wandered through a series of compact and low-beamed rooms filled with antique Hopi and Navajo rugs, silver and turquoise jewelry burnished with age, new baskets woven in traditional geometric designs, Western hats, boots, and framed paintings of the Grand Canyon in its various guises: at sunset and sunrise, under snow, in the delicate greenery of spring. Nowhere was there a rendition of fog. As the couple moved through the tightly packed space, they became aware of a quiet but intense conversation in what was clearly an upstairs display area. It was Ginger Wolfe and D.C. Irving.

"But Dad forgave him in the end, D.C. . . . He chalked it up to Will's youth. I remember him saying, 'When these whippersnappers make mistakes, they do it big. Folks can get hurt.' "

"A snake in the grass is still a snake in the grass."

"I appreciate your concern, but you don't need to dislike Will on our account. Tommy and I have gotten past any harsh feelings, or even disappointment . . . If the real estate deal—"

"Your father should never—"

"But we're *happy* having careers . . . which we probably wouldn't have if Will and Dad hadn't—"

"Happy? Arranging luxury tours for the idle rich?"

Belle frowned as she stared up at the ceiling. There was rising bitterness in D.C.'s voice. Obviously, teaching golf to "the idle rich" could be deemed equally belittling.

Ginger Wolfe changed the subject. "Were you able to track down John, and tell him what happened? Gwen's still in a bad way."

"I tried his cell phone, tried his home and office, but like Joe says—when John's beating the bushes for investors, nothing gets in his way . . ."

The words faded as footsteps carried the speakers out of range. Belle turned a corner trying to follow the disappearing words, and ran smack into Tommy Wolfe. "Hunting for a perfect gift for your hubby?" he asked.

"Well . . . no, not exactly."

"You must be hunting for something . . . Or are you just out for a stroll? Maybe go down to the trail, and see the spot where poor Will took the plunge? Everyone else seems to want to go down and ogle it."

Rosco stepped out from behind a rack of post cards and inserted himself between his wife and the twin. Tommy Wolfe's demeanor seemed surprisingly hostile and aggressive.

"Well, well, if it isn't our resident private eye?"

Rosco looked at Tommy and then briefly at Belle before returning his gaze to the twin. "It seems like you're not too upset about Mawme's passing . . . Maybe that's because of the real estate deal your father—"

"That was years ago," Tommy interrupted with a curt wave of his hand. "It's all . . ." His cell phone rang, checking his speech, and he made a quick grab for his breast pocket. "Yes?" He glanced at his watch. "I'm on my way." He folded the phone and replaced it.

"Problems?" Rosco asked.

"My sister. She's expecting me."

"But she's upstairs with D.C. . . ." Belle began.

"Well . . . Yes . . . That's where I was to meet her." He checked his watch once more. "Gotta go."

Rosco watched him leave, then also frowned in confusion. "Tommy used the word 'hunting' twice," he said.

"So I noticed."

"And why would his sister phone him if she's upstairs?"

"Beats me." Belle looked up at the ceiling. There was no sound from the second floor.

"Do you have Mawme's puzzle with you?"

She removed it from her purse, and handed it to him. He studied it for a minute, then shook his head. "GOT YOU HUNTER . . . There's no way that's coincidental, as Evans suggested."

"I agree."

"I think it's time for another little chat with Hunter Evans. But first, I'd like to have a look at the spot where Mawme fell. Do you feel like taking a walk? Before it gets dark?"

Belle considered saying, "Gee, I was hoping to catch the second half of the game," but realized the joke might back-fire. Instead she slipped her arm through his.

THE quarter-mile walk along the Rim Trail, from Hopi House to the spot where Will Mawme had slipped, took less than ten minutes. The trail passed through a carved rock archway made ominous and spectral by the fog. Walking beneath it, Belle and Rosco emerged at the site of the "accident" and were greeted by a Day-Glo yellow sign stating: DANGEROUS OVERLOOK—DO NOT ENTER. In case the words weren't dire enough, the Park Service had attached a smaller sign that cautioned: DON'T GO NEAR THE EDGE, FOOTING MAY BE DANGEROUS.

"I don't know how much more warning folks need," Rosco observed. He moved near the signs, and peered down. "It's a sheer drop."

"Be careful, Rosco. The footing's slippery."

"I know . . . It's hard to tell what happened here. I don't know if these disturbances in the snow were the result of a struggle, or if they were left by the rescue workers."

"Well, one thing's for sure," Belle said, pointing to a set of narrow tire marks in the now crusty snow. "Our friend Joe Conrad has been here. Those lines were left by a wheelchair."

"But when? He could have only come down here this morning—"

At that moment a ten-year-old boy darted out from beneath the archway, running backward as he shouted, "Hey, cut it out, mister!" Heedless of the presence of other people, the boy barreled into Belle, causing her to lose her balance, and making them both, adult and child, collapse in a tangled heap. And as she fell, she kicked Rosco's boots, sending him skidding helplessly toward the edge of the precipice. His arms flailed through the air, desperately searching for something, anything, to grab on to. And then he was gone, disappearing from view—leaving Belle flattened on the ground, panting in pain and terror as everything she loved vanished from sight.

She cried out Rosco's name as the boy scrambled to his feet, still oblivious to the fact that where there were now only two people there had once been three. "I'm sorry, lady, but it wasn't my fault I bumped into you . . . Some guy started throwing snowballs at me. Hard . . . I was just trying to get away . . ."

"Rosco!" Belle moaned while tears flooded her eyes.

"I said I was sorry, lady." The boy reached down toward Belle, and as he did, Hunter Evans stepped from the stone arch.

"That's the man!" The boy pointed. "He's the one who started pelting me with snowballs. It wasn't my fault I knocked you down."

"Come on, kid," Hunter laughed, "you were having a good time . . . No harm done." He looked at Belle. "Where's your hubby? Hope he hasn't decided to hike to the canyon floor. The footing isn't the best."

Belle stared up at Hunter. "He fell . . ."

A soft groan arrested further speech. It was followed by: "Oh, man, my shoulder—"

Belle leapt up and stumbled toward the canyon's edge. At the base of the metal pole supporting the warning sign was Rosco's gloved left hand. A second later his right hand swung up and grabbed the pole. Belle moved closer to the rim as Hunter and the boy took a quick step backward.

"Stop, Belle!" Rosco shouted. "I don't want you to fall. I can pull myself up. I've just wrenched the heck out of my shoulder . . ." He grunted as his hands gripped the pole, and he began to work his boots against the cliff's rugged face. After a good deal of struggling, he reached level ground and began pulling himself away from the crumbling and treacherous edge.

The boy yelped as Rosco clambered to his knees. In the dense air, he looked like a creature arisen from an open grave.

"Fancy seeing you here, Hunter," Rosco said as he caught his breath.

Evans's face darkened. "Look, I was just having some fun with the kid. How was I to know you were going to get hurt?"

Rosco and Belle regarded him. Mawme's sinister message—GOT YOU HUNTER—suddenly ricocheted through their brains.

"Accidents happen, Polycrates," Evans snarled as if in response to the unspoken accusation.

"Just like your name 'accidentally' showed up in your friend Will Mawme's crossword. Just like he 'accidentally' fell and died."

"Get a life, Polycrates." Hunter Evans began to move away.

Rosco gritted his teeth. "That doesn't exactly answer my question, does it?"

Evans turned, his expression grim. "Which would be what, Polycrates? Because if you or your little wife here are alleging I—"

"What can you tell me about Tetlee Isaac?" Rosco's words made Evans's eyes turn blank and wary.

"Who?"

"Tetlee Isaac."

"Never heard of him."

Rosco massaged his shoulder. "Well, he's bound to turn up, and he's bound to talk; he obviously talked to Will Mawme. It's only a matter of time before we find him."

Hunter seemed about to speak, but instead snapped his mouth shut, and stalked away, while Belle grabbed Rosco and squeezed him as tightly as his injury allowed. "I was so scared. I thought . . . I thought . . ." She was now trembling. He held her close until she stopped. Finally she looked up at him and said, "Who's Tetlee Isaac?"

"As I was falling . . . Well, you know how they say people have their lives flash before them when something like that happens?"

"Yes."

Rosco chuckled, although the sound was rueful. "In my case it was that darn puzzle . . . Let me see it again."

Belle retrieved the crossword.

"Here," Rosco pointed, "on the parallel diagonal, starting at 50-Across, and going up . . . ?"

Belle read, "CHANCES ARE I . . ."

"Right. Add that to the message you spotted earlier, and finish it up with the corresponding diagonal beginning at 69-Across."

Again Belle read aloud, "CHANCES ARE I . . . GOT YOU HUNTER . . ." Her finger continued tracing the lines. "MET TETLEE ISAAC . . . This is what you saw when you were falling off the cliff?"

Rosco shrugged. "There's no explaining how our minds work. Maybe it's from hanging out with you—"

"As it were," Belle said. She hugged him tighter.

"Anyway, what I realized is that it's clear this Tetlee Isaac person has something on Hunter Evans, and that he shared it with Mawme. And looking at this message, I'd say that Mawme was either threatening to expose Hunter, or possibly blackmail him. Although I'd like to think a prosecutor wouldn't be into blackmail."

Belle glanced at the puzzle once more, then back to Rosco. "That makes sense," she sighed, "except for one thing."

"What's that?"

"I believed Hunter when he said he'd never heard of Tetlee Isaac. I think he was telling us the truth."

"I know. That's what bothers me, too. I think he was also."

BEFORE going down to dinner that evening, Rosco attempted to locate the mystery man Isaac by phoning information services in a number of cities: Flagstaff, Prescott, Phoenix, Tucson, Santa Fe, Albuquerque, and even Las Vegas, but there was no listing for Tetlee Isaac in either downtown, suburbs, or outlying communities.

"That was a futile effort. Not even an unlisted number," he said as he dropped the phone into its cradle for the last time. "I'd love to know who this guy is."

Belle thought. "I'll bet someone in our little crosswording group knows . . . And that's the same person who pushed Mawme into the canyon."

"Problem is: No one seems to be looking at this thing as a homicide."

Belle sat on the bed next to Rosco. Their shoulders were touching, but slouched in defeat. "Do you think the state of Arizona will even consider classifying Mawme's death as something other than 'accidental'?"

"Since he was a federal prosecutor, they're bound to look into it, Belle, but to be honest, there's no evidence that it wasn't an accident. It's just the crossword that arouses suspicion."

She nodded slowly. "And tomorrow morning we—and the puzzle gang—go home."

"Meaning tonight's the last chance to get them all together and flush our criminal—*if* such a person exists." Rosco stood and slipped on his sports jacket; he grunted in discomfort as he did so. "Shall we retire to dinner, my lovely? See what's cooking? Stir the pot? See who can stand the heat."

"You're awfully brave, Rosco. Did I ever tell you that?"

"Flattery will get you everywhere."

Belle gazed at him. "I love you."

"Keep it up."

BEFORE entering the dining room, Rosco and Belle took a few moments to get coordinated on their approach. If they had a chance to uncover a murderer, they'd need to be on the same page, and be well aware of the other's intentions. They agreed not to mention Tetlee Isaac again, opting to see if any of the other puzzlers had been able to detect the hidden message within Mawme's grid. The wild card would be Hunter Evans. If he began talking about their acrimonious meeting on the trail, the plan could be foiled.

As usual, the group's table had been set for ten people. Out of respect for their fallen comrade, they decided to leave the head of the table empty, with Mawme's place card resting on the serving plate. Belle was seated at the other end of the table, with Rosco three seats down on her left. The twins sat opposite one another, farthest away from Belle, Joe Conrad positioned his wheelchair across from Rosco, Jean sat next to him, D.C. across from her, and Gwen and Hunter took the chairs on either side of Belle.

During the appetizer, salad, and main courses the conversation was appropriately subdued. Polite stories were recycled from past gatherings. Naturally, Will Mawme's name was attached to each. Some of the tales brought grave smiles, others quiet tears. Belle and Rosco never mentioned their suspicions of foul play, and everyone seemed comfortable with the notion that the death had been accidental. Dessert was served and consumed, and the group of nine retired to the upstairs lounge for coffee by the fire.

"I'm sorry your event had to conclude on such a terrible note," Belle said after everyone had found a seat. "I know you were counting on a special puzzle from me, and I have copies of the crossword I designed to send home with you. It just didn't seem appropriate, given the circumstances, to—" She broke off her speech and took a small sip of coffee. "However, I just remembered an old game I used to play as a child. It's lighthearted, and I thought it might be a pleasant diversion for our last evening together."

Belle lifted a decorative bowl from the mantel, and dropped eight folded slips of paper into it. She smiled. "I'm going to let Rosco play as well, if that's okay with you? We need an even number of players."

Joe Conrad chortled, "The more the merrier. Who knows? He may show us all up."

Belle cleared her throat. "Here are the rules: On the pieces of paper are the names of eight famous people and a number from one to four. That means that there are two number fours, two number threes, etc. Your partner will be the person who has your corresponding number. Any confusion so far?" She looked at the group; all, including Rosco, indicated their comprehension.

"At my signal, everyone reaches into the bowl and selects a name; and from that moment on, no one can say a word. It's basically a form of charades. Each player must get his or her partner to say the celebrity's name through hand gestures and pantomime. No speech allowed. I'll time each couple, and the one who gets both names solved in the least amount of time wins."

"What do we win?" Ginger Wolfe asked with a fair amount mistrust in her voice.

"That's a surprise. Any other questions?"

Again, everyone shook their head.

"Okay, then." Belle walked among the puzzlers with the bowl of names. "No one unfold his or her paper until I give the signal."

After all had taken a slip of paper, Belle returned the bowl to the mantel. "Okay, when I count to three, open your papers. One . . . two . . . three."

The seven puzzlers quickly unfolded their slips while Rosco and Belle studied their reactions.

Hunter Evans smiled broadly and said, "I see how this game works."

Belle shushed him and started to say, "No talking," but was interrupted by Gwen Beckstein uttering a harsh and frightened cry:

"I didn't have anything to do with it!" she wailed. "It was all John's idea! He said he'd take care of the whole thing."

Everyone spun toward her; and she shrank back under their piercing stares. "Don't look at me like that! It was John! It wasn't me . . ."

"It was John who what?" Tommy Wolfe demanded, but Gwen Beckstein slumped in her chair and seemed not to hear him.

"I just never thought he'd go after Will . . . but once Isaac was dead, John was . . . he was . . ."

Belle and Rosco remained silent, while confusion swept the others.

It was Hunter Evans who picked up on the ruse. He pulled the slip of paper from Gwen's hand and read aloud: "Tetlee Isaac."

"I have the same name," D.C. Irving interjected.

"I'd venture to say we all do," Hunter replied as he eyed Belle and Rosco.

"Who is he? Or I suppose I should say, who *was* he?" Tommy asked. His bewilderment was complete; he glanced at his sister, who returned his gaze with equal bewilderment.

"It was all John's doing," Gwen said through tears that were fast turning into heavy sobs. "I never met the man."

Rosco and Belle remained on the sidelines as Hunter

pushed Gwen for answers. "But what could your husband have had against Will Mawme, Gwen? Other than these annual get-togethers, they hardly spoke to one another."

"Hardly spoke?" Gwen nearly screamed. "What difference does that make? Mawme was a federal prosecutor, and Isaac was threatening to turn state's evidence. We were going to jail! Can't you see that?"

"No," Hunter pressed, "I don't."

Gwen looked from face to face. Expressions ranged from incredulity, to horror, to pity. Again tears began to stream from her eyes. "Tetlee Isaac was from Hong Kong . . . He represented a group of investors that held a forty percent share in Sandstone Estates, our land development project . . ." She nodded meaningfully at Hunter. "The investment you were considering participating in."

"That you and John own sixty percent of."

"That's just it," Gwen said. "We don't own a thing. John brought in straw partners. I asked him not to . . . I told him it was way too dangerous the way he was doing it . . . a money-laundering scheme with some men from Texas— drug money . . . But John insisted it was a sure thing, 'risk free,' he said until he could scramble 'something more legit' . . . But then Tetlee Isaac caught on. He wanted out, and threatened to blow the lid off the entire project, which would have meant—" The words died in her throat. She lowered her head in grief. "So John . . . he . . . he decided he'd have to 'remove' Isaac before he contacted Will, and then—"

"But according to Mawme's puzzle," Hunter protested, "it would seem he and Isaac had already spoken . . ." He stared at Gwen's bent head. "And why did my name appear in CHANCES ARE I GOT YOU HUNTER?"

"You're wrong in both instances, old man."

The new voice drew all eyes to the oak-beamed doorway. In it stood John Beckstein. He was handcuffed. He stepped into the room followed by two Arizona state troopers, then looked at Gwen and said, "You just don't know when to keep your mouth shut, do you, my dear?"

Hunter Evans glowered at him. "What do you mean by 'wrong in both instances'?"

Beckstein looked at his wife as he spoke, his expression strangely calm for a man who had committed not one but two homicides. "Will Mawme never met Tetlee Isaac, Gwennie. You and I were in error on that point. No, our indefatigable prosecutor simply learned that the man had died, grew suspicious of me and my lovely, if overly talkative wife, and decided to do precisely what Ms. Graham did— flush us out." John Beckstein turned to Belle and bowed slightly. "Well done, my dear . . . Mawme would have been proud of you." He turned back to Hunter Evans. "You interpreted the message incorrectly. It should have been read: CHANCES ARE I GOT YOU—HUNTER MET TETLEE ISAAC. Mawme was covering himself by implying that you—a prospective investor—had also met with Isaac. And he was setting you up as bait. The mistake he made was assuming that Isaac's killer would go after you first . . . And believe me, Hunter, if your guest of honor and her husband hadn't been near that stone archway this afternoon, you would have joined Will Mawme on the canyon floor. I was right behind you."

The taller of the two troopers pulled a set of handcuffs from his belt and crossed over to Gwen. "I'm afraid you're under arrest, ma'am. There's a car waiting for us downstairs."

Rosco reached into his sports jacket and withdrew a small tape recorder. He removed the tape and handed it to the trooper. "This might come in handy."

"Thank you, sir." The troopers then escorted John and Gwen Beckstein out of the room.

"Well," Tommy said at length, "I don't know about the rest of you . . ." He looked at his sister, who gave him a wan smile. ". . . but I was *Spellbound.* After all, John was beyond *Suspicion* . . . As for you, Hunter, you definitely seemed like *The Wrong Man* . . . But hey, give a guy enough *Rope* . . . Beyond a *Shadow of a Doubt,* it ended up being just a *Family Plot.*"

"Clever," Belle replied wearily, "but I'm afraid I'm exhausted." She took Rosco's arm. "So, we'll bid you all a good night."

As they stepped through the oak doorway, Tommy couldn't resist one last shot. "Ahhh . . . *The Lady Vanishes!*"

Cross Stitch

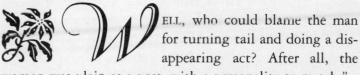ELL, who could blame the man
for turning tail and doing a dis-
appearing act? After all, the
woman was plain as a post, with a personality to match."

"Weezie! Honestly! That's a shameful way to speak about
the dead." This was DiAnne Thomassen speaking; the
woman she was addressing was her equal in years, if little
else. Like DiAnne, Louise "Weezie" Walters was in her mid-
fifties, but where DiAnne was tight-lipped and regimental—
in both bearing and outlook—Weezie was unabashedly,
even cheerfully, rotund, and favored dramatic apparel of her
own concoction. In this case, the outfit was vaguely Christmasy: a long, emerald-hued skirt under a flowing silk blouse
of rose and orange. A wide scarf of nile green completed the
picture.

At present, Weezie was a painter. She "adored experimenting with the Arts" and, in the past, had tried her hand at being a sculptor, a ceramicist, a photographer, and a jazz vocalist. She was also the self-styled "bad girl" of the group, a role she relished.

"Must I to refer to the woman as *attractive,* Dee?" Weezie complained with a loud, delighted cackle. "Or how about *striking?* That one's always been a favorite of mine; although I prefer to save it for show horses. Your notion of political correctness has gone way, way, *way* too far, my gal. You know as well as I do that Prudence Pierce was butt ugl—"

"Girls . . . girls . . ." Sara Crane Briephs intervened, while DiAnne, or Dee (she loathed the college-vintage nickname), silently ground her perfect teeth, and then inadvertently stabbed her finger with a tapestry needle. The mistake, or perhaps Weezie's insurrection, brought tears to her eyes.

"Ouch," DiAnne grumbled.

"A stitch in time, Dee . . . You gotta learn to lighten up," Weezie goaded as Sara again urged a gentle:

"Let's remember why we've gathered here this afternoon, ladies. This is church business we're about."

Only Kate Stamp bent closer to her needle and the unfinished church pew kneeler in her hand. Kate was the youngest of the five women seated in the sitting room of White Caps, Sara Briephs's ancestral home. She was as good and affectionate as DiAnne was primly proper; or as Weezie was defiantly dramatic. Kate had just turned thirty-one, a young thirty-one, hopeful and beaming with generosity and joy. Her husband and two small boys received large daily dollops of love; and her soon-to-be third baby would as well. Kate's secret heart, however, held a small rebellious streak, making her a private admirer of Weezie's free and easy style. Not that she imagined she'd ever have the courage to be so audacious.

"I never met Mrs. Pierce," said the fifth woman, Martha Leonetti. Martha was the head waitress at Lawson's Coffee Shop in downtown Newcastle, Massachusetts. In DiAnne's eyes, Martha, blue-collar, blunt-spoken, and street-savvy, was not an appropriate "fit" for a group she believed, first and foremost, to be a private club for "society ladies." Naturally, Weezie wholeheartedly disagreed with what she considered to be "Dee's outrageously snooty behavior." Besides, Martha was privy to more local gossip than all the others combined; and dishing the dirt was another of Weezie's favorite diversions.

"Lucky you, Martha." Weezie rolled her eyes, sucked in her pink and fleshy cheeks as if drinking lemon juice straight. "A real pill, if there ever was one!"

"Weezie!"

"Oh, c'mon, Dee. Don't tell me you really liked the old bat!"

"I admired her very much, Weezie. She was a pillar of society, and a kind benefactress to many of Newcastle's organizations."

"Hah, you sound like you're putting her up for sainthood. *Admire* and *like* ain't the same thing at all. Not at all."

Weezie had nearly topped her on that point, but DiAnne countered with a swift, "We wouldn't be gathered here, creating something beautiful for our worship services, if it hadn't been for the late Mrs. Pierce's skillful needlework and design sense—"

"Cross stitch . . . old cross patch," Weezie interjected. "Besides, if you want to get technical, my kneeler features a poinsettia—which we all know is a poisonous plant. Think about that! And Sara's is an angel's trumpet, a *datura,* which is even worse!"

"Many flowering plants are unwholesome—"

" 'Unwholesome,' my eye! The *datura* was once used in India to execute criminals! And swiftly, I might add. In South America, it was given to wives and slaves about to be buried alive with their lord."

"You're simply spouting that witches' brew stuff you're so fond of."

"DiAnne! This is historical and scientific fact, not witchcraft! The angel's trumpet will send you back to where you came from in the blink of an eye."

Kate stifled a giggle while Sara cautioned an admonishing, "Girls! You sound as if you've returned to grade school. Besides, I'll thank you to remember that Prudence Pierce was of my generation. So take care when you use the word 'old.' "

"But *you* are old, Sara," Weezie said with a sweeping gesture of one hefty arm. "Old, indomitable, fabulous! When I'm eighty plus, I plan on being exactly like you. Regal, unflappable—"

"You've got your work cut out, Weezie, if 'unflappable' is your intention," DiAnne shot back, although a smile was beginning to soften her disapproving features. Despite their differences, DiAnne and Weezie had been close friends for many, many years.

For several long moments, the five women focused on

their task: stitching new covers for the church kneelers. The canvas upon which each individual design had been painted rested on their laps, a soft blue gros-point background circling a brightly hued petit-point flower. When finished, DiAnne's would be a yellow iris, Martha's a purple hyacinth; Kate's a pink and mauve anemone; Weezie's a red poinsettia; and Sara's the elegant—if lethal—*datura* or angel's trumpet. The covers already completed lay rolled at the bottom of a wood chest filled with cedar chips. It had been Prudence Pierce's wish that her final gift to her church should remain uninstalled until each of the pieces of needlepoint was finished. One hundred cushions of which these five were the last. Fourteen years since the donor's death, and more than a thousand hours of stitchery by an ever-changing group of parishioners.

Heads bent in concentration: Sara's white hair impeccably coiffed; Kate with curling, brown locks that never quite stayed put; Martha's "do" an intrepid bottle-blond shellacked into a time-warp beehive; DiAnne's a discreet silvery bob; and Weezie's current color a glittering plum red. According to her, the shade was "this year's fashion statement . . . in Paris." Like her career choices, like her wardrobe, like her vivid folk-art jewelry, Weezie believed wholeheartedly in experimentation.

Beyond the heads and deftly moving fingers, the room echoed with purposeful calm: chintz-covered chairs, antique mahogany furniture, alabaster lamps with beige silk shades, aged Oriental carpets, a cheery fire sizzling below the carved marble mantle, a Delft clock sitting squarely upon the marble's white surface, while outside the winter afternoon windows lay a leaden sky, a "snow sky" that made the viewer happy to remain indoors.

"What *really* happened to *Mister* Pierce?" It was Kate who asked the innocent question. "I know some of the gossip, of course, but—"

"Hightailed it," was Weezie's immediate reply. "Just like all the stories say. No ifs, ands, or buts . . . Disappeared off the face of the earth, as far as anyone can tell . . . In his defense, though, it could not have been easy married to the 'heiress'—"

"She never referred to herself as such," DiAnne interposed with some austerity. "Never."

"But that's what she was, Dee! She let all and sundry know she had more money than G—"

"You inherited wealth yourself, Weezie, let's remember. It's not a crime."

Weezie bristled; her red hair followed suit. "I've never been in Prudence Pierce's category, not by a long shot. And I've never needed *lucre* to lure a man to my bed—"

"Or three . . ." DiAnne countered.

"Three *husbands,* Dee . . . Anyway, I'm proud of my femininity—"

"Proud is one thing—"

"We have no way of knowing if Prudence's financial position affected her choice of a spouse . . . or he of her," Sara interrupted; her tone was severe, clearly indicating it was time to move on to another subject. But Martha decided to weigh in anyway.

"Well, it would me," was her blithe riposte. "I would have given my eyeteeth to marry a millionaire. I still would, though I'm guessing I just might have missed my chance. Not many high rollers amongst the Lawson's lunch crowd."

"Well, there's always the breakfast bunch," Weezie offered.

Martha chuckled. "My age might be against me, too . . . Well, what are you gonna do?" She sighed, although the sound was more amused than rueful.

"Play the lottery?" Weezie proposed.

"There ya go!" Martha laughed. "Then I'd be a gazillionaire in my own right. Without any rich hubby to cater to."

"So . . . so, Phillip deserted his wife?" Kate asked after another moment of silence. Her expression was troubled; she was a person who felt others' pain swiftly and deeply.

"Yes." It was Sara who answered. Her voice was somber. She put down her needlework; her blue eyes were hard and unforgiving. "The rumor was that Phillip ran off with the nanny. He and Prudence had a son, an only child, late in their marriage—"

"Yes, yes, that's right . . ." put in Weezie. "I vaguely remember the story, now . . . No one spoke about the kid, though . . . something wrong with him from birth. He had to be institutionalized—"

Kate gasped. All faces turned in remorseful dismay toward her very pregnant belly.

"I didn't mean—" Weezie began, but Kate, wide-eyed, cut her off:

"Is he still . . . institutionalized?"

Again, it was Sara who spoke the difficult truth. "Prudence's son died, dear, long before his mother."

Kate's eyes swelled with tears as the other women exchanged guilty and uncomfortable glances, then DiAnne looked toward the windows. "Goodness! It's begun to snow. Look at it! A real blizzard. That's not at all what the newscasters were predicting."

With that, all the lights flickered, then failed completely.

"Oh, not again!" Sara said. "I suppose the entire of Liberty Hill will be out of power—as usual. When, in heaven's name, will they finally embrace the twenty-first century and bury those infernal electrical wires?"

LIKE the remainder of the house set high on the hill overlooking Newcastle and its harbor, the spacious kitchen at White Caps was a compilation of long-past eras: late-nineteenth-century glass-fronted cabinetry, an early-twentieth-century zinc-topped worktable, a deep copper sink circa 1930, wood countertops crisscrossed with decades' worth of knife pricks and scrapes, and a gleaming 1940s white cast-iron stove outfitted with compartments for warming plates and rolls. The "newest" piece of equipment was an electric toaster—already a classic, purchased in 1956.

Lit now by hurricane lamps and candles, and with the gas stove heating milk for cocoa while its broiling rack turned homemade bread into cinnamon toast, the room was the most comforting place imaginable.

"It's coming down in positive sheets," Weezie observed from the window. She was letting DiAnne and Kate "do the honors" at the stove while Sara and Martha retrieved first a set of gilt-rimmed cocoa cups that had belonged to Sara's mother, then a silver serving tray, silver spoons, linen napkins, a creamer, and the sugar bowl for those who required extra sweetening—accoutrements the staunch old lady felt indispensable when presenting warm liquid refreshment. Never for Sara a mug, a packet of instant "chocolate mix," or hot water straight from the tap.

"Which means the hill road will be sheer glass within the hour," Sara observed. "If it isn't already."

"Oh . . ." Kate murmured.

Sara frowned in self-rebuke. "How inconsiderate of me, dear. Of course, you must get home to your little ones. I should have sent you on your way at once . . . We'll call your Andrew; he can fetch you. I don't want you driving in this." Sara retrieved the phone from the wall but found that service had gone the way of the electricity. "Oh, one of you girls will have to use your portable—"

"It's all right, Sara. I'm okay to stay." There was something hollow and tentative in Kate's tone that made the other women take immediate note. But they did so out of the corners of their eyes, then just as furtively turned their pensive glances in Sara's direction.

"I don't mind calling Andy if you don't want to be pegged as a 'weather wimp,' " Martha offered.

The quaint expression would normally have brought a smile to Kate's face. This time it did not.

Uncharacteristically, it was DiAnne who spoke the reassuring words all were thinking. "What happened to Mrs. Pierce's baby won't happen to yours, Kate . . . You have two beautiful, healthy boys already; and you've told us the doctor indicated 'clear sailing' ahead."

Kate didn't reply at first. When she did, it was to avoid

the subject altogether. Again, this seemed unusual. "This is so nice . . . being with you all . . . It's like school days." She sighed. "Cocoa and conversation. I feel as if I should have on my pj's and slippers."

"If the snow keeps up, we'll all wish we'd brought pj's," Weezie wisecracked.

"Back to the drawing room and fireplace?" Sara asked while Martha stated a pragmatic:

"Lucky thing your furnace isn't electric, Sara."

"That's where you're wrong in your assessment, Martha," chuckled Weezie. "It's lucky the ancient thing doesn't still burn *coal.*"

"Jest all you wish about my parsimonious ways, ladies. But let us remember to give thanks that we *have* heat—and that I was persuaded to install an emergency generator gizmo to aid the furnace's electrical starter thingy . . . Now, there are plenty of nightclothes and wool dressing gowns upstairs, though they may smell a tad of mothballs."

"Oh, I love you all to pieces!" Kate gushed. She hugged Sara, who sent a perturbed glance in the direction of the other women before ordering a gentle: "We should have our cocoa before it gets cool. If someone would carry the hurricane lamps, and another the candles . . ."

"THIS is the game," Weezie announced as she put her cocoa cup on the mantle and placed another log on the fire. "We go around the circle, each person fessing up to their most embarrassing moment. Whoever has the worst story wins."

"That would be me," Sara announced with an airy smile

as her guests gazed at her in wonderment. "I was thirteen. My father had put me on a train to New York. I was traveling alone to spend the weekend with a great-aunt who lived there. On Beekman Place, which had a very grand ring to a child from coastal Massachusetts . . . I'd never gone such a distance on my own hook before, and I was dressed for the occasion: a good dress hat—brown leghorn straw, I recall . . . gloves with three pearl buttons—"

"You still wear dressy hats and gloves, Sara," interrupted Weezie. "Are you sure you were only thirteen?"

"Hush," murmured DiAnne.

"Yes. It was warm weather, and I was bare-legged—"

"Being bare-legged ain't so terrible." Weezie chuckled. "That's how everybody dresses nowadays, Sara, along with exposed navels, in case you—"

"Hush, Weez, will you?" DiAnne protested. "Let Sara finish."

"It's an important element of the tale, Louise," the old lady continued. "The other element is that I had a most recalcitrant pair of combinations—"

"Combinations?" Kate asked.

"Panties, dear . . . Originally, a term for a one-piece undergarment covering both top and bottom . . . We didn't use the word 'panties' in those antediluvian times. I don't know why . . ." Sara squinted as she remembered; two bright pink spots lit up her cheeks. "My hips had not yet . . . Well, I was a bit of a beanpole then, if you can believe it. At any rate, it was an undergarment that began slithering downward as I walked through the train . . . until, with a whoosh, it fell down around my ankles."

Martha's blue-shadowed eyes were wide. The notion that the august old lady could ever have experienced a disconcerting situation was inconceivable.

"What did you do?" she asked.

"Walked away from it."

"Walked away?" Martha persisted.

"Stepped out of the wretched thing and continued down the aisle as if I were merely stepping over an annoying piece of trash."

"What did the other passengers do?" Martha asked.

"I have no idea. I never looked back . . . But I'll tell you I could have walked off that moving train, and all the way to Beekman Place if I'd been able . . . As it was, I simply marched forward, car by car . . . When I reached the door leading to the Pullman coach, I stopped, and took a seat. I don't think my spine hit the chair's back during the entire journey . . . And my leghorn straw? Oh, it felt like nettles clinging to my scalp."

Weezie was now laughing so hard she cried. "Marched forward and never looked back. That's so like you, Sara."

"What choice did I have?"

"I can think of plenty, starting with a squeal and a hasty retreat to the nearest ladies' room . . . though if it had been me, I would have ended in an undignified tumble with my bare rump exposed to the horrified onlookers."

"Precisely why I kept going," Sara stated. "And it's why I never keep a stitch of clothing that has an old or fraying elastic waistband."

"Well, that certainly alters our image of you, Sara," DiAnne said. "The next thing you know you're going to tell us that you and Prudence Pierce broke wind in public."

Sara had also started to laugh. "What Prudence did, I'm afraid, I have no record of. As for me . . ."

Laughter became infectious then, the easy mirth shared by people comfortable with one another. It was Kate who interrupted.

"We shouldn't make fun of Mrs. Pierce," she ventured. "After all, she—"

"You're right," Martha agreed. "You have to walk a mile in someone else's shoes—"

"Or 'combinations,'" Weezie added with a mischievous grin, but the jest ended in a sudden thump of snow spilling from the roof to land in a pile on the formal boxwood hedge that ran the length of the house. There was a pinging crack as branches split and broke under the weight. Every head turned toward the sound, then all five women stood and walked to the windows.

Before them, the landscape was solid white. The green of the rhododendrons and azaleas was buried; firs bent under cover of snow so deep it looked like icing slathered on by a giddy and unsupervised child; only the pruned and bare rosebushes, poking up above the drifts, showed a hint of black, but every crevice of every branch was daubed with frothy ice. What had become of the trees and shrubbery more distant to the house was impossible to tell.

"No one's going home tonight," observed Weezie, "not unless it's by strapping on snowshoes or taking a sled down the hill."

"You'll want to phone your boys and Andrew." Take-charge Sara turned to Kate as she spoke. "I know *my* husband was totally useless when it came to the culinary arts—"

"The boys aren't with Andy." Kate's words, spoken quickly, had a curious and almost atonal breathlessness. "They're at my sister's . . . for a few days . . ."

The other women waited; no one moved or allowed themselves to appear disconcerted by the news.

"I was feeling . . . well, just anxious, you know . . . and with the baby coming so soon . . . my sister thought it might be a good idea for me to have a little time to myself . . . Breathing room, she said."

"That's a sensible notion," Martha began. "Husbands and wives need to spend time alone together; especially with a new one in the oven."

But the unhappy look on Kate's face indicated such was not the case.

"Andrew's not home, either . . . is he," DiAnne prompted.

"No." Kate seemed about to say more. She opened her mouth, shut it, then began to weep.

Above her bent head, her friends looked at each other, a wordless fusion of comfort and support in one communal body.

"How long has Andrew been gone?" DiAnne asked.

"Only a day this time."

"This time?" It was DiAnne who reiterated the words the others echoed in silence.

"It's not what you think!"

"We're not 'thinking' anything at all, dear," Sara soothed. Her quick glance at Weezie sent her back to the fire and a fresh log piled upon the glowing embers; toward Martha, to a chair pulled toward the rekindled blaze, a pillow patted and waiting for Kate to sit; toward DiAnne, to a box of tissues.

Without being aware of her friends' guidance, Kate found herself in the chair, the other women hovering close by. She looked up, her face strained, miserable. "It's my fault he's gone."

Weezie's expression clouded in indignation. "Your fault? It's not your—" She stopped what might have become a diatribe when she felt Sara's fingers lightly touch her arm.

"Why do you say that, Kate?" Sara asked.

"I've been so . . . so needy . . . so, well, whiny and complainy . . . and work isn't going well for him . . . and the kids, well, little boys can be so rambunctious . . . and then Andy can't relax when he comes home . . . and I can't make the house as nice as he wants it to be . . ."

Again, Weezie was on the verge of interrupting; again, Sara soundlessly held her in check:

"And where is Andrew now, dear?"

"At his brother's . . . I think." Kate's voice had sunk to a near-whisper.

"You 'think'?"

"That's what he told me, Sara, but . . ."

"But what?" This time Weezie's ire couldn't be contained.

"Well, what if he's having an affair? What if that's why he's gone off on his own? What if he's like Prudence Pierce's husband?" Kate began to sob.

DiAnne proffered the box of tissues; her own expression

had taken on a peculiar combination of stoicism and grief. "He's not having an affair, Kate."

"You don't know that, DiAnne!"

"Yes, I do. Because if he were, you would have guessed. Unfaithful spouses always give themselves away. Maybe that's because deep down they want to be caught."

The others now regarded DiAnne, who lifted her chin in a perfectly typical gesture of resourcefulness and reserve.

It was Weezie who gave voice to what all were thinking. "Oh, Dee, I didn't know . . . I'm so sorry . . ."

But Weezie's effort at conciliation was interrupted as Kate burst into fresh tears. "See! The same thing happened to DiAnne!"

DiAnne stroked her hair. "Don't cry, sweetheart . . . It wasn't my husband who cheated—it was me."

SUPPER consisted of serious "comfort foods": Ritz crackers piled with peanut butter and jelly (who knew Sara could have a stash of peanut butter?); canned tomato soup thickened with real cream; ginger snaps (wasn't ginger a root—like carrots or turnips?); a quart of butterscotch ice cream that almost didn't make it past the five-spoons-in-a-pot category; a block of Vermont cheddar cut in fat chunks; popcorn cooked in an ancient pot on top of the stove and drizzled with an entire stick of melted butter; warmed cider stirred with cinnamon sticks—and all eaten piecemeal. Sara had decreed that rules did not apply, not for the entire snowbound night. To bolster the dictum, she'd produced camphor-scented nightclothes and antique dressing gowns, slippers, and wool socks. Along with this "girls' dorm" attire, the edibles seemed a perfect fit.

Outside, it continued to snow and snow and snow, but once Kate had "beamed in" with her sister and kids, and been assured the two boys were "happy as clams at high tide," no one at White Caps cared what the weather did.

However, to the group sitting—or rather, lounging—around the zinc-topped kitchen table with the remnants of the feast, it became increasingly obvious that DiAnne's confession, as well as Kate's admission, wouldn't be as easily dispensed with as the blizzard. Conversation about who preferred "crunchy" peanut butter to "smooth" or visa versa was wearing thin; the ice cream was gone; the popcorn had been reduced to a few charred and unpopped kernels. It was time to take the bull by the horns. It was DiAnne who did so.

"I'm afraid I dropped rather a bomb back there." She hesitated, frowning, her lips a tight and solemn line. For a moment it seemed as though the old DiAnne, the prim-and-proper lady, was about to reassert herself. "My behavior isn't something I'm proud of . . ." Again, she stopped. No one else stirred except Martha, who oh-so-gently set down a spoon.

"Oh, I could find a lot of excuses . . . I was young . . . I didn't feel Frank 'valued' me . . . He was working at the bank almost nonstop . . . I didn't have enough to occupy me—and goodness knows, I need to keep busy, as I'm sure you're all aware." DiAnne allowed herself a thin, wry smile. "Or maybe I merely wanted excitement . . . I was raised to value self-denial, to behave politely in all circumstances, to remember I was a 'lady' first and foremost . . . Maybe, I was simply trying to rebel . . ." The words trailed off.

"Which isn't always a bad thing, Dee," Weezie offered after a moment. "You have to flutter your wings a little if you want to learn how to fly."

DiAnne turned to her. "True for you perhaps, because you've never hurt anyone. I did, though. I hurt a very decent man."

"But you're still married to the same guy, Dee. What you did obviously didn't cause irreparable pain or damage."

"He's a good person, Weez. He forgave me."

Weezie's eyes narrowed into slits. The notion of begging absolution didn't sit well with her.

It was Martha who addressed the heart of the matter. "Forgiveness from another person is one thing. But perhaps you haven't forgiven yourself?"

DiAnne's sad eyes gazed into Martha's. She shook her head. "I can't."

"But isn't that the lesson we're supposed to learn?" Kate asked. "Isn't that what we always hear in church: Forgive others . . . love each other as you do yourself?"

Weezie attempted a teasing chuckle. "I'm not going to address *that* subject."

"Well, yes, Kate," Martha added slowly, "that's what we're taught: to love each other as we much as we do ourselves . . . But . . . but I'm not really certain I love *myself* all that much."

"Oh!" Weezie said. "I thought I was the only person who felt that way."

"Me, too . . ." Kate admitted in a tiny voice.

DiAnne sighed and lowered her head while Sara offered her own well-seasoned view:

"My grandmother used to talk a lot about courage—not love or forgiveness, which probably speaks volumes about her New England forebears . . . Courage, she liked to tell me, was the most important of all the emotions, because without it, you could sustain no other: neither love, nor compassion, nor joy . . . She said that it took courage to live, to overlook unkindnesses, to turn the other cheek—"

A rumbling roar interrupted the speech; the floor beneath the kitchen seemed almost to shake. "The furnace!" Sara exclaimed. "This does not bode well."

IN the dark and oily-smelling basement, the five women stood in a semicircle staring at a furnace that no longer pulsed with heat and ruddy light. The emergency generator "gizmo" had apparently shut down as well; and all dials and gauges now pointed to a discouraging and chilly "zero." Weezie swung a hurricane lamp nearer for a closer inspection of the controls. "Yep, it's given up the ghost all right . . . and chose quite a night, too. Lucky it's not one of those subzero cold snaps we get. The water pipes would be in serious trouble."

"Well, we can bunk together in the sitting room," Sara decided. "Keep the fire well banked . . . Carry down twin mattresses and eiderdowns from the guest rooms. One of us can camp out on the sofa."

As they turned back to the stairs, Kate murmured a pensive: "Given up the ghost . . . Wouldn't it be amazing if this entire event, the storm and everything, were being arranged by Prudence Pierce's ghost? Because I feel . . . I feel we were *supposed* to spend this time together . . . becoming real friends . . . not just women who like to sew together. And it does seem to me as if someone could be orchestrating the whole thing."

"Poor Prudence," Sara said after a moment. "I don't imagine she had any true friendships."

"Aren't we the lucky ones, then?" Martha offered as they passed through the dark and rapidly cooling house.

KATE awakened during the night, sat up, drew her quilt over her shoulders, and stared at the flickering fire. Around her the others were sleeping peaceably: Sara, snoring ever so softly, an old lady's genteel and guttural wheeze; Martha mumbling something that sounded like a rote recitation of Lawson's breakfast menu.

Kate's eyes began to roam the room and the nestled forms stretched out at the bases of Chippendale tables and tallboys. It was an incongruous sight: snoozing bodies littering White Caps' formal sitting room. Kate smiled to herself, then realized suddenly what made the picture so special. Moonlight raked the floor, spilling across torsos and heads. Moonlight! Which meant that the snow had stopped. Quietly, she extricated herself from sheets and eiderdown, and tiptoed to the cold windows.

Outside, the world glittered. Reflecting the sky, the lawn and gardens spiraled headily past trees and bushes, creating eddies of coal-black shadow against a white so glaring it almost hurt the eyes. It was a magical landscape, and it conjured up for Kate her favorite childhood poem, *The Night Before Christmas*. She smiled, thinking of how her eldest tried to recite it, changing: "gave the lustre of mid-day to objects below" to "*obich deblow*." Then the happy expression turned downward in worry and confusion. She leaned closer to the icy glass, her breath creating crystals on the pane.

DiAnne stood beside her with an arm firmly around her shoulders before Kate realized anyone from the group was awake. "You love Andrew, don't you, Kate?"

"Oh, yes!"

"And he loves you." DiAnne's words were half-question, half-statement, but Kate's response was merely to hang her head further.

"Okay, let's step back a bit. Why wouldn't he love you?"

"Well . . . I'm not a terrific housekeeper . . . and suppers with the kids can get pretty chaotic—"

"Is Andrew a neatnik?"

Kate smiled. "Not by a long shot."

"Okay . . . What makes you think he values tidiness?"

"His mom's house—"

"You're his wife, not his mother."

Kate thought. DiAnne continued. "And what about those 'chaotic suppers'? Do you enjoy them?"

"Sure!"

"Really?"

"Well . . . most of the time . . . but sometimes . . . well, there's nothing anyone can do about it. Kids are kids."

"That's where you're wrong, Kate. Kids *are* kids, but you and Andrew are adults; and adults and children can have very different ways of enjoying themselves . . . Now, I've got a suggestion. You can take it or leave it, but here goes: Why don't you and Andrew organize a once-a-week outing; call it a date—"

"But we're married, not—"

"A date to see a movie, maybe grab a bite to afterward . . . a time that will be yours as a *couple,* not solely as parents."

"But what if Andy doesn't want to? What if he keeps leaving because he truly doesn't want to be bogged down with a family?"

"My hunch is that he doesn't know how to talk about what's bugging him. Maybe he's feeling overwhelmed but doesn't want to burden you. I'm not saying he's right by pulling a disappearing act—not by a long shot. I know how much his behavior troubles you but, well, what can I say? Men aren't as comfortable as women with expressing their emotions—even if they can identify them. And that's a big *if.*"

Kate pondered DiAnne's words while the older woman continued. "You and Andy are both young; you've got a lot on your plates. You're going to have a good deal more soon. If I'm wrong about his motives . . . well, let's cross that bridge *if* we come to it. And I don't believe we will." She gave Kate's shoulder a squeeze.

"How did you become so smart, DiAnne?"

"Trial and error, and a *lot* of mistakes—including the biggie I mentioned earlier."

"But you make everything seem so easy . . . No, that's not exactly what I mean . . . You—and Sara—you both appear so self-assured, so capable, so *steady*. No one on the outside would ever guess you were hurting."

"Generations of Waspy New Englanders . . . It's how we were raised: demure manners, carefully modulated voices, ready smiles—which is a crock, really, 'cause no one ever realizes you're in need or in pain."

Kate nodded. "And you and Frank?"

"What I did was a long time ago. Strange to say, but I feel it made me a better wife. It certainly made me appreciate my husband a heck of a lot more . . . I guess that's the basis of any good marriage: valuing—and honoring—your spouse. Giving one hundred percent on both sides."

"I'm glad Prudence Pierce brought us together."

"And I'm glad you love your family, and that you show it, Kate. Because at the end of the day—or of a life—that's what counts. It may be the only thing that does."

Kate hugged DiAnne, who hugged her back. "I'm sorry our needlework is almost finished, DiAnne. We won't have a reason to be together—"

"We'll just have to find a new excuse."

MORNING found Sara's sitting room cold, but awash in the ebullient sunlight that follows a snowstorm, that follows any storm.

"Brrr . . ." Weezie said, rising slowly. Still wrapped in her quilt, she placed another log on the fire's fading embers, then broke up kindling, rolled newspapers, and proceeded to build the blaze.

"Coffee? Coffee, please; someone find coffee . . ." Martha

muttered. Her entire head was under her covers.

"Don't tell me you're not a morning person," Weezie wisecracked. "What time do you get into Lawson's each morning? Five-thirty—six A.M.?"

"*When* I'm working," Martha parried. "When I'm not, I can be a total slug . . . And anyway, I don't go on duty until I'm *well* fortified with major doses of caffeine."

"I'm afraid breakfast means braving the elements," Sara announced, pulling herself erect in her habitually straight-backed pose. "The kitchen's going to be frigid. Ditto: the foyer and butler's pantry. But the gas is on—I hope."

Kate and DiAnne volunteered to fetch food for all while Weezie and Martha began picking up pillows and stacking mattresses. When they came to the needlework kneelers that had been discarded the previous evening, they held them up to Sara.

"Return them to the chest, don't you think?" she advised. "Our fingers are too cold to work properly. We'll be a mess of pinpricks."

Weezie and Martha rolled the five kneelers together, and opened the chest's wood lid.

"Oh, the smell is so comforting," Weezie sighed. "So old-fashioned . . ."

"I never thought I'd hear you taking comfort in the past, Louise," Sara jested. "What next?"

Weezie merely raised her eyebrows, bent her body closer to the woolly needlework, and reached for a handful of finished kneelers. "A rose . . . a daffodil . . . snowdrops . . . oh, this is nice: love-in-a-mist. No poisonous leaves or petals here." She unrolled four more. "Clematis . . . marigold . . . a

petunia . . . stock . . . Oh, how I adore the scent of stock . . .
It reminds me of my mother . . ." Weezie pulled out additional kneelers, oohing and aahing over them in a manner
quite unlike her "bad girl" image, then sat back upon her
heels. "There's a puzzle stuffed into one . . ."

"They're all a puzzle, if you ask me," Martha said. "Canvases dotted with holes that don't become real pictures until
you finish stitching them."

"No, I mean a real puzzle. A crossword thing . . ." Weezie
chuckled as she lifted paper gone yellow and brittle with
age. "Here, Sara, you're good at these, aren't you?" Weezie
laughed again. "It probably contains a message detailing
Mrs. Pierce's instructions on the care and cleaning of tex-
tiles. Maybe the old—maybe our 'benefactress' had a playful
side after all . . . No, no, wait, better yet; maybe it reveals
where she stuffed the body of her 'disappearing' husband!"

"Well, if our crosswording friend, Belle Graham, were
here," Sara said with a kindly smile, "she'd certainly jump
to that most outrageous of conclusions."

Kate and DiAnne returned with a tray brimming with
coffee and fresh-made muffins to find Sara, Weezie, and Martha huddled together on the sofa, filling in the crossword.

"Ah, Weezie's found herself another game," DiAnne observed with a smile. "Let's hope it doesn't produce any more
embarrassing moments . . . I suggest you three put that
aside and have a pick-me-up first."

Martha was the first to rise, her nose drawing her toward
the steaming coffee. "Manna from the gods. You two have
certainly come up with a feast. Homemade muffins, too?"

"From scratch. Credit Kate on that."

Weezie dropped the puzzle on the side table, as DiAnne approached her and Sara with two cups of hot coffee. Before they could take a sip, a pounding sound echoed from the brass knocker on White Caps' front door.

"My goodness," Sara said with a start. "Who on earth could that be?"

"There's only one way to find out." DiAnne set the coffee down and walked into the foyer. She returned a moment later, followed by Kate's husband, Andrew.

"I figured you ladies must have gotten yourselves snowed in," he said. "I borrowed Ricky's four-by-four, so I was able to make it up the hill. That drive's a sheet of ice, though. We're going to need to get a plow and a snowblower in here if you have any hope of getting your cars out before April Fools' Day."

Kate walked over to him; she didn't say a word, just gazed at her husband in love, relief, admiration, and joy.

"I missed you . . ." Andy said, then turned and faced the other women. "Umm . . . I'd be glad to offer you all a ride home, but, ah, there's really only room for two in the truck."

"We understand completely," Weezie announced. "Don't you worry, Andy, we'll work something out." She pulled her cell phone from her purse. "We'll call in the Marines."

"Thanks."

Kate grabbed her coat from the entry hall closet, and the two of them nearly ran out the front door.

"Well, well, well," Weezie said, "who would have guessed? The loving husband cometh with the snowman!"

Martha took another thoughtful sip of coffee, then added a quiet: "Oh, please, if Andy Stamp was having an affair, I would have heard about it months ago." Then she slowly turned her gaze on DiAnne, whose mouth fell open:

"You knew about—me? Back when?"

"Might have."

"Oh, Martha! And you never . . . ! And I was so . . . ! Oh, I'm so sorry!" There weren't enough words to sufficiently express DiAnne's chagrin.

Martha held up a hand. "No apologies necessary." She smiled at DiAnne and then Weezie, and finally looked toward Sara, who was resolutely completing Prudence Pierce's crossword.

Finished, Sara passed the puzzle to the others, who read it in silence.

"Poor woman," Weezie finally said. "And to think that all this time—"

"No," DiAnne and Martha countered, almost in unison; and DiAnne followed it with, "There's nothing poor, or even remotely sad or tragic, about these words. In fact—"

"In fact, it's a most 'prudent' of messages," Sara added. "And timely . . ."

"Aren't we lucky to be the ones who found it?" DiAnne concluded. "Rather than someone else."

ACROSS

1. Tie
7. With 7-Down, what & when partner
10. Smoke's end
14. Run out
15. Owned
16. A woodwind
17. Thought; part 1
19. 23-Across output
20. Irate
21. MFA studies
22. Georgia or Virginia
23. It sounds just like you
24. Thought; part 2
27. Golf item
28. Consumed
29. Thought; part 3
35. Offer
38. Author Haley
39. Morning moisture
40. Study; with up
41. Gents
42. Source of thought
46. Sup
47. Army bed
48. Thought; part 4
53. Arrest
56. Assert
57. Log or sode lead-in
58. Large book
59. Thailand neighbor
60. Thought; part 5
63. Rifle rounds
64. Summer drink
65. Less ornate
66. Kill off
67. Bro's sib
68. Kitchen gadgets

DOWN

1. Taunt
2. Yoke attachment
3. Steeple
4. Following in or out
5. Mrs. Custer portrayer
6. Adored one
7. With 7-Across, what & when partner
8. Waste maker
9. Lyric poem
10. Tuxedo neckwear
11. Sub
12. Molar
13. Phone or vision lead-in
18. Laugh sound
22. Fill
24. Constant Comment
25. Layer
26. "The bestest"; abbr.
27. 48-Down locale; abbr.
29. Emoter
30. Corida cheer
31. Inker
32. Germany for short
33. 35-Down, in Hawaii
34. Possess
35. Feather stole
36. Roadhouse
37. _____Moines
40. Iota
42. Relaxed
43. Siouan
44. Scolding sound
45. Garden tool

🌴 *A Stitch in Time* 🌴

46. Microphone inventor
48. Historic mission
49. Ruth's mother-in-law
50. Music-man Giuseppe
51. Duelers
52. Spanish aunt
53. _____Dame

54. Brown stone
55. Miller & Reingold
56. Adorned
58. Despot
60. Auto fuel
61. Cooking meas.
62. Gov. watchdog grp.

The Answers

Digger's Challenge

🌴 Poetic Justice 🌴

1 P	2 O	3 L		4 V	5 A	6 C		7 B	8 O	9 O		10 H	11 A	12 M
13 A	P	E		14 I	C	I		15 E	F	T		16 E	L	I
17 R	E	G	18 R	E	T	C	19 O	N	F	20 O	U	N	D	S
21 I	N	G	O	T		22 A	D	E		23 E	R	R	E	D
24 A	S	I	T		25 D	I	A			26 N	I	N	A	
27 H	E	N		28 F	A	S	T	29 S		30 I	T	T		
	31 A	G	32 E	33 D	I	S	T	H	34 E	35 L	E	V	E	E
	36 T	E	N				37 R	A	T					
38 T	39 H	40 E	C	L	41 A	42 Y	43 I	S	F	R	44 E	45 S	H	
46 R	I	P		47 L	A	M	P	S			48 N	A	49 G	
50 A	D	I	51 T		52 N	B	A			53 H	A	R	I	
54 P	E	C	A	55 N		56 K	U	R	57	K	A	P	P	A
58 P	O	U	R	S	59 W	E	E	T	60 N	E	S	S	O	N
61 E	U	R		62 E	W	E		63 A	N	N		64 T	O	T
65 R	T	E		66 W	I	S		67 N	E	T		68 O	N	S

Still, Man Wasted Talent

B	U	S	■	A	B	C	■	B	A	T	■	E	L	F
A	N	T	I	G	U	A	■	L	I	E	■	N	E	O
D	I	A	M	O	N	D	S	A	R	E	■	J	A	R
G	O	L	F	■	G	E	T	B	Y	■	H	O	S	E
E	N	L	■	S	E	T	A	■	P	A	Y	T	V	
■	T	H	E	S	T	O	N	E	S	A	R	E		
■	E	S	S	O	■	E	T	C	H	■	B	A	R	
N	N	E	D	I	S	C	O	■	T	L	C	■		
A	S	O	■	O	U	S	T	■	J	O	E	Y	■	
I	N	W	I	T	H	T	R	E	V	O	R	■		
N	A	B	O	B	■	E	L	O	N	■	L	E	M	
T	R	O	D	■	T	R	E	V	I	■	M	E	G	A
Y	E	O	■	Q	U	I	T	E	C	L	E	V	E	R
O	R	T	■	E	T	C	■	R	E	A	L	I	S	T
U	S	S	■	D	U	E	■	S	S	S	■	S	T	Y

195

There's a Hitch!

A completed crossword puzzle grid. The filled letters read:

M	I	T		I	N	A		A	N	I		A	P	T

Row by row:

- M I T ▮ I N A ▮ A N I ▮ A P T
- A D O ▮ N E V ▮ B E N ▮ R E O
- D A R ▮ T H E W R O N G M A N
- ▮ ▮ N H L ▮ R A I N E R
- P A C O ▮ S S R ▮ A E R ▮ S A C
- T R U S T E E ▮ E T D ▮ T A B
- A F R I C A ▮ N N E ▮ E A R S
- ▮ T N U ▮ B U D ▮ M S G
- H A A G ▮ S H E ▮ N I C E S T
- I H I ▮ T U T ▮ R E B U F F S
- C A N N O N ▮ J E T ▮ D R O P
- ▮ Y O D E L S ▮ M O I
- C A T C H A T H I E F ▮ G A S
- O O O ▮ O E R ▮ D E A ▮ H S T
- G L O ▮ T S E ▮ E L S ▮ T A P

🌿 *A Stitch in Time* 🌿

1 T	2 O	3 S	4 S	5 U	6 P		7 W	8 H	9 O		10 B	11 U	12 T	13 T
14 E	X	P	I	R	E		15 H	A	D		16 O	B	O	E
17 A	B	I	D	E	T	18 H	E	S	E		19 W	O	O	L
20 S	O	R	E			21 A	R	T		22 S	T	A	T	E
23 E	W	E		24 T	25 H	R	E	E	26 F	A	I	T	H	
		27 T	E	E				28 A	T	E				
29 H	30 O	31 P	E	A	N	D	32 L	33 O	34 V	E		35 B	36 I	37 D
38 A	L	E	X			39 D	F	W		40 B	O	N	E	
41 M	E	N		42 C	43 O	R	I	N	44 T	45 H	I	A	N	S
		46 E	A	T				47 C	O	T				
	48 A	49 N	D	L	50 O	51 V	52 E	T	H	E		53 N	54 A	55 B
56 C	L	A	I	M		57 E	P	I		58 T	O	M	E	
59 L	A	O	S		60 G	R	E	A	61 T	62 E	S	T	B	E
63 A	M	M	O		64 A	D	E		65 S	P	A	R	E	R
66 D	O	I	N		67 S	I	S		68 P	A	R	E	R	S